ALSO BY KHALED KHALIFA

In Praise of Hatred
No Knives in the Kitchens of This City

DEATH
IS
HARD
WORK

KHALED KHALIFA

Translated from the Arabic by Leri Price

FABER & FABER

First published in the UK in 2019 by
Faber & Faber Limited
Bloomsbury House, 74–77 Great Russell Street
London WC1B 3DA

This paperback edition first published in 2020

First published in the United States in 2019
by Farrar, Straus and Giroux
175 Varick Street, New York 10014

Originally published in Arabic in 2016 by Nawfal, an imprint of
Hachette-Antoine, Lebanon, as *Al mawt aamalon chaq* (موت عمل شاقلا)

Printed and bound by CPI Group (UK) Ltd, Croydon CR0 4YY

All rights reserved
Copyright © 2016 by Hachette-Antoine
Translation copyright © 2019 by Leri Price

The right of Khaled Khalifa to be identified as author of this work has been asserted in
accordance with Section 77 of the Copyright, Designs and Patents Act 1988

This is a work of fiction. Names, characters, places and incidents either are the product of
the author's imagination or are used fictitiously. Any resemblance to actual persons,
living or dead, events or locales is entirely coincidental.

*This book is sold subject to the condition that it shall not, by way of trade or otherwise, be lent,
resold, hired out or otherwise circulated without the publisher's prior consent in any form of
binding or cover other than that in which it is published and without a similar condition
including this condition being imposed on the subsequent purchaser*

A CIP record for this book
is available from the British Library

ISBN 978–0–571–34605–9

2 4 6 8 10 9 7 5 3 1

CONTENTS

DEATH IS HARD WORK

IF YOU WERE
A SACK OF CUMIN

Two hours before he died, Abdel Latif al-Salim looked his son Bolbol straight in the eye with as much of his remaining strength as he could muster and repeated his request to be buried in the cemetery of Anabiya. After all this time, he said, his bones would rest in his hometown beside his sister Layla; he almost added, *Beside her scent*, but he wasn't sure that the dead would smell the same after four decades. He considered these few words his last wish and added nothing that might render them the least bit ambiguous. Resolved to be silent in his last hours, he closed his eyes, ignoring the people around him, and sank into solitude with a smile. He thought of Nevine: her smile, her scent, her naked body wrapped in a black abaya as she tried to float like the butterflies they were collecting. He remembered how his eyes shone at that moment, how his heart had thudded, how his knees trembled, how he carried her to the bed and kissed her greedily, but before he could recall every moment of that "night of immortal secrets," as they'd secretly dubbed that particular evening, he died.

Bolbol, in a rare moment of courage, under the influence of his father's parting words and sad, misted eyes, acted firmly and without fear. He promised his father he would carry out his instructions, which—despite their clarity and simplicity—would hardly be easy work. It's only natural for a man, full of regrets and knowing he'll die within hours, to be weak and make impossible requests. And then it's equally natural for the person tending to that man to put on a cheerful front, as Bolbol was doing, so as not to let the dying man feel that he has been abandoned. Our final moments in this life aren't generally an appropriate time for clear-eyed reflection; indeed, they always find us at our most sentimental. There's no room left in them for rational thought, because time itself has solidified and expanded inside them like water becoming ice. Peace and deliberation are required for reviewing the past and settling our accounts—and these are practices that those approaching death rarely take the time to do. The dying can't wait to fling aside their burdens, the better to cross the *barzakh*—to the other side, where time has no value.

Bolbol, later, regretted not having stood up to his father. He should have reminded his father how difficult it would be to carry out his instructions given the current situation. There were mass graves everywhere filled with casualties who'd never even been identified. No *'aza* lasted more than a few hours now, even for the rich: death was no longer a carnival people threw in order to demonstrate their wealth and prestige. A few roses, a few mourners yawning in a half-empty living room for a couple of hours, someone reciting a sura or two from the Qur'an in a low voice . . . that was all anybody got.

A silent funeral is a funeral stripped of all its awe, Bolbol thought. Rites and rituals meant nothing now. For the first time, everyone was truly equal in death. The poor and the rich, officers and infantry in the regime's army, armed squadron commanders, regular soldiers, random passersby, and those who would remain forever anonymous: all were buried with the same pitiful processions. Death wasn't even a source of distress anymore: it had become an escape much envied by the living.

But this was a different story. *This* body would be big trouble. Thanks to a fleeting moment of sentiment, Bolbol had promised to bury his father in the same grave as Bolbol's aunt—whom he had never even met. He had thought that his father would ask for some sort of precautionary guarantee of Nevine's rights to the family home, seeing as they had married only recently. The building had been reduced to a shell in an air raid, leaving intact only the bedroom where his father had passed his last days of love with Nevine before leaving the town of S with the help of opposition fighters . . .

Bolbol would never forget that scene. His father had been immaculate when the fighters brought him to Damascus from the besieged S; it was clear that they had taken good care of their comrade, this man who'd chosen to stay with them through more than three years of siege. They bade him an affectionate farewell, kissed him warmly, and saluted him. After enjoining Bolbol to be good to his father, they vanished down a well-guarded side road leading back to the orchards surrounding the village. Abdel Latif's eyes were gleaming as he tried and failed to raise his hand to wave to his comrades. He was exhausted and starving, having lost more than half his body weight; like everyone living under the siege, he hadn't eaten a full meal in months.

Now his body was laid out on a metal stretcher in a public hospital. A doctor told Bolbol, "People are dying in droves every single day. Be happy he managed to reach such an old age." Bolbol wasn't quite able to follow the doctor's instructions to be cheerful at his father's death, although he could grasp what was meant. He felt as though he were suffocating beneath the weight of his new predicament. The city streets were a wasteland after eight in the evening, and he had to move the body tomorrow morning, after it was released and before midday. A large consignment of soldiers' corpses would arrive at dawn from the outskirts of Damascus, where the fighting never stopped. There wouldn't be room for his father at the local morgue for long.

When Bolbol left the hospital, it was almost two o'clock in the morning. He decided that his father's last request ought to apply to the rest of the family, too, not just Bolbol himself: everyone ought to be equally responsible for carrying out Abdel Latif's last wish. He looked for a taxi to take him to his brother's house after successive attempts to phone him had failed. He considered texting Hussein the news, but it would have been beneath contempt to let him know that way. Things like that had to be said face-to-face, and the pain shared equally.

The soldiers guarding the hospital waved him toward the nearby Deraa Station—he would find a taxi there. Bolbol decided not to think too much about the gunfire he could hear. He put his hands in his pockets, quickened his pace, and swallowed his fear.

Even a short walk on a winter night like this was extremely hazardous: the patrols never stopped, and the streets were teeming with faceless gunmen. The power had been cut off in most quarters, and concrete blocks were piled high in front of the improvised "offices" set up by the national security branches, occupying most roads. Only residents could possibly have known which routes were permissible and which forbidden. From a distance, Bolbol saw a few men gathered in a circle around an upturned gas can in which some firewood had been set alight. He guessed that they were mostly taxi drivers trapped by the closure of various roads, waiting for dawn so they could go home. The last glimmer of his courage had almost flickered out by the time he found a taxi driver—listening serenely to Um Kulthoum on the car radio—willing to take him. Bolbol quickly reached an understanding with him and didn't argue with the fare that he was quoted.

They didn't talk at first, but after a few minutes Bolbol wanted to try and exorcise his fear. He told the driver that his father had died an hour ago in the hospital, of old age. The driver laughed and informed him that three of his brothers as well as all of their children had died a month before in an air strike. Both went quiet after this; the conversation was no longer on an even footing. Bolbol had been expecting a little sympathy from the driver. Nevertheless, the man behaved honorably and didn't drive away until he was sure that Bolbol was safe. Hussein opened the door, and when he saw Bolbol standing there at that time of the morning, he knew what had happened. He hugged his brother affectionately, led him inside, and made him some tea. He asked if Bolbol wanted to wash his face and promised to take care of everything that still needed to be done: finding a shroud, making the burial arrangements, fetching their sister, Fatima.

Bolbol felt himself become lighter and braver, his worries lifting away. He no longer cared that Hussein had completely ignored their father when Abdel Latif was in the hospital; the important thing was that Hussein wouldn't follow this up by abandoning him now. Bolbol was confident in his brother's ability to manage this sort of situation. Hussein had meandered around among several professions before taking a job as a minibus driver, and if nothing else this meant he'd gained considerable experience dealing with the state bureaucracy, and he had contacts all over the place. Without delay, Hussein dismantled the two seats immediately behind the driver's and rearranged them to form a shelf for the body to lie on. He said, "We'll lay the body here. That way there'll be enough room for everyone else to travel comfortably." He meant Bolbol and their sister, Fatima, but if their in-laws wanted to come along, too, well, they wouldn't be in the way. This idea was soon rejected, though: they couldn't imagine that anyone else would still harbor any sense of duty toward this man whose corpse would have to negotiate hundreds of miles to reach its final resting place.

By seven o'clock, Hussein had finished all the arrangements for the journey. He had brought their sister over from her house and blanked out the scrolling signs on his minibus, which he ordinarily used to work the Jaramana line. With the help of an electrician friend, he improvised an ambulance siren out of its horn. He also bought an air freshener, which he supposed would be needed on the long journey, and didn't forget to call another one of his friends who was able to supply four large blocks of ice. Despite the difficulty of his requests, his friends all had woken before dawn, offered him their condolences, and helped Hussein to arrange everything for the journey. The only thing still left to obtain before they could be on their way was the signature of the hospital director, who wouldn't be in before nine o'clock. They parked in front of the hospital gate to wait for him, but a morgue official asked them to remove their father's body immediately, as the freezers already needed to be emptied out to accommodate the fresh shipment of corpses that had just arrived, now simply heaped on the floor.

Bolbol didn't dare accompany Hussein when he went into the morgue. The corridors were full of the dark, sad faces of men and women waiting to receive the bodies of their loved ones. The orderly indicated that Hussein should search the southern side of the morgue, and Hussein almost threw up as he opened a fridge chock-full of bodies. He'd almost lost hope by the time he found his father's body; hundreds of corpses had been lost and forgotten in this chaos. It was clear that his father hadn't been dead for long. Hussein slipped three thousand liras to the official so that the orderly would be allowed to help him wash and shroud the body in the filthy bathroom reserved for the dead, which no one bothered to clean. The scene in the hospital was horrifying. Officers were pacing the corridors and shouting curses against the opposition fighters. Troops in full combat gear were wandering around aimlessly, smelling of battle. They had brought their friends, either wounded or killed, and dawdling there was their only way to escape or postpone returning to battle, where death would no doubt find them as well. Death always seemed near in this chaos.

Back at the van, Hussein arranged his father's body in such a way that he wouldn't have to see him and be distracted whenever he looked in the rearview mirror. He told Fatima to be quiet, even though she hadn't spoken a word, but she only sobbed harder. Hussein had always enjoyed ordering her around, ever since they were children, and Fatima obeyed him without argument; complying with her brother's demands gave her a sense of equilibrium and security. Hussein was furious at Bolbol when he noticed him leaning against a nearby wall and smoking as if he didn't have a care in the world. He slammed the door of the van and went back to the hospital gate to wait for the director, who had to sign the death certificate before the body could officially be released. It wasn't exactly the place to make small talk, but he couldn't help asking a woman, also waiting, if she knew when the director was expected. She shrugged and turned her face away. Hussein didn't bother trying to speak to anyone else, although he hated waiting in silence; he believed that a little chat would have alleviated their misery. He could feel the tension and anger hidden in the eyes of the petitioners who were packed in all around them.

At nine o'clock, the director arrived and signed the certificate. Immediately, Hussein told Bolbol to get in the bus and instructed Fatima to cover the body with the blankets that he had brought from his house. And also to shut up.

Hussein informed his siblings that removing the body had cost them ten thousand liras, adding that he was recording every expense in a small ledger. Without waiting for their reaction, he began strategizing about the quickest way out of Damascus. The streets would be clogged with traffic at this time of the morning, and the many checkpoints would be jammed; it might take hours to clear the city limits. His calculations proceeded based on his experience spending whole days in traffic as a minibus driver. The road through Abbasiyin Square would be best, although the security checkpoints had a particularly bad reputation in that area. Even *trying* to cross Sabaa Bahrat Square in downtown would be a disaster, he told himself.

So Hussein decided to chance Abbasiyin Square and tried to follow close behind a proper ambulance. He was stopped at the first checkpoint, which wouldn't allow him to travel along the main road, but he was still able to make some headway along an alternate route. The faux siren he'd installed in the minibus was no use whatsoever—no one made way for him. Amid the crowds and the chaos, Hussein recalled how funeral processions used to be respected back in peacetime—cars would pull over, passersby would stop and cast you genuinely sympathetic looks . . .

A row of additional ambulances suddenly descended on him, all heading out of the city. Inside each one were soldiers accompanying coffins; Hussein could see them through the small windows in their back doors. He tried to sneak in between two of the vehicles, but an angry yell and a cocked weapon from one of their furious occupants returned him to the line of civilian vehicles. When the last ambulance in the queue pulled up alongside the minibus, it slowed down, and a soldier leaned out of the window to spit copiously on him and berate him in the foulest possible language. Hussein looked at the spittle moistening his arm and was flooded with rage. Rage and then the desire to weep. Bolbol kept quiet and averted his eyes so as not to increase his brother's embarrassment. Fatima, for her part, no longer felt like crying; she was surprised at how few tears she had shed, all things considered. She decided to postpone expressing the remainder of her sadness and loss until the burial, which would no doubt be the most emotional part of the farewell to her father.

Since childhood, Hussein had been in the habit of memorizing entire pages of the cheap almanacs published by Islamic philanthropic organizations, containing famous sayings, aphorisms, verses from the Qur'an, and prophetic Hadith, and he used them in everyday speech to give his audience the impression of his being well read. He used to believe that he hadn't been created to live on the margins of life as a mere observer, but at that moment, looking at the deluge of vehicles inundating Abbasiyin Square, he felt terrifyingly powerless; he couldn't find an appropriate aphorism to break the strident silence dominating his brother and sister, yet he wanted very much to make them forget that he had just been spat on. He tried to remember something or other about life and death but couldn't come up with anything better than "Tend to the living—the dead are already gone." He didn't like it, however, because of how often the line was quoted by cowards justifying retreat. And in any case, today it might be a different matter—better to tend to the dead; after all, they now outnumbered the living. He went on to muse that they would all surely be dead in the not-too-distant future. This thought had given him exceptional courage over the previous four years. Not only had it served to increase his stoicism day by day, but he was far better able to withstand the many insults he received from checkpoint soldiers and Mukhabarat in the course of his work if he bore this thought in mind, since it allowed him to subscribe to the view that anyone who gave him a hard time would probably be dead today or tomorrow, or by next month at the latest. Not that this was a particularly pleasant notion, but it was an accurate one, and each citizen had to live under the shadow of this understanding. The inhabitants of the city regarded everyone they saw as not so much "alive" as "pre-dead." It gave them a little relief from their frustration and anger.

The bus crawled painfully toward the hundreds of vehicles flooding Abbasiyin Square. Three Suzuki pickup trucks with hoisted flags gleamed ahead of the siblings, heading in their direction; elderly men were standing in the open backs and trying to clear the road. One of them yelled through a bullhorn, loud and clear, "Martyrs, martyrs, martyrs!" He followed this up with "Make way for the martyrs, make way for the martyrs!" But no one cared. The Suzuki trucks approached Hussein's minibus and tried to escape the traffic. Hussein noted aloud that they were coming from Tishreen Military Hospital and added that there was no transport to take the poor to their graves. Bolbol couldn't take his eyes off the man with the bullhorn. He stared at him until he was lost from view.

There was no getting away from death, Bolbol told himself. It was a terrifying flood drowning everyone. He recalled the days when the regime still bothered to put effort into the funerals it staged for its fallen. On television, an ensemble would play some song written especially for the state's many martyrs, and on every coffin there would be a large bouquet bearing the name of the commander in chief of the army and the armed forces (who was also the president), another in the name of the minister of defense, and a third in the name of the deceased's comrades in arms in his squadron or department. A female anchor would announce the name, function, and rank of the martyr, and this would be followed with a shot of the family declaring how proud they were, how glorious it was, that their son had been martyred, faithfully laying down his life for the nation and the Leader. Always those two words— "nation" and "Leader." And yet, after several months, the band, the bouquets, and the flag disappeared; so did the female anchors crowing about the penniless boys martyred for their loyalty to the nation and the Leader; and so did all reverence for the word "martyr." Bolbol looked at the city as it dwindled around them. He remembered how passionate his coworkers had been when they used to tell their horror stories: searching for bodies that had been lost or buried improperly, through hospitals stuffed with corpses . . . Tracking down the remains of a loved one had become hard work—

even more so when a family, immediately upon being informed of the death of a son, was forced to go over to the battlefield and dig through a mass grave, or else among various devastated buildings and the iron skeletons of tanks and burned-out guns. But the bloom went off even these sorts of stories, eventually, and no one bothered to tell them anymore. The exceptional had become habitual, and tragedies were simply mundane—perhaps that was the worst part of this war. In any case, though, as Bolbol looked at his father's corpse, he felt a certain degree of distinction; at least *this* body was being cared for by its three children and not left to the mercy of the elements. He almost told Hussein and Fatima about their father's last moments—in fact, he was surprised that he hadn't already done so—but instead lay back, convinced that there would be plenty of time on the long drive to talk over the exploits of the departed, to recall a past that had never been particularly unhappy.

Hussein was still annoyed at himself. The thousands of sayings and aphorisms he'd spent twenty years memorizing had proved useless in the face of a bad traffic jam—but he refused to let his defective memory get the better of him. He repeated a few sayings on different topics, just to keep in practice: aphorisms on unfaithfulness and hope and the betrayal of friends. He considered this a useful exercise; these sayings might be required sometime soon, and they needed to be primed and ready. He called a few lines of Ahmad Shawqi to mind and recited them vehemently, enunciating majestically: "Crimson freedom has a door / Knocked by every blood-stained hand . . ." The following line only came back to him with difficulty: ". . . he will ever dwell among the pits." But no, he had mixed up Shawqi's poem with one by Shaby, "If One Day the People Wish to Live, Fate Must Respond." But this combination pleased him; if anything, it struck him as fortuitous that he'd accidentally blended two poems with very different meters and rhyme schemes. He had in fact read these lines dozens of times on the pages of his almanacs and liked them very much; he used them to shame cowards who preferred the regime to any unrest. He repeated both incomplete lines in a murmur as if in lament for his revolutionary father.

Bolbol paid no attention; he was content with the three previous months he and his father had spent talking everything over. Fatima understood the recitation as a belated reconciliation between Hussein and their father. She wanted to thank God out loud for this miraculous resolution, but Bolbol's heavy silence made her hesitate, and she decided to wait for a more suitable opportunity to voice her opinion on the long rift between father and son. True, their estrangement had gone through many different stages, and occasionally each man had even approached the other, trying to turn over a new leaf, but no matter what, their relationship never regained its original, cloudless perfection from the time when Hussein had been the spoiled favorite.

The soldiers at the last checkpoint within the limits of Damascus made do with a cursory glance over their papers and allowed them to pass. Many corpses were leaving the city today, and just as many were coming in. The sight of them was abhorrent to the mud-spattered soldiers; the bodies heralded their own imminent end, which they naturally wanted to forget. Hussein didn't look at his watch. He heaved a sigh of relief; he had been delivered from the traffic of Abbasiyin Square, and Damascus was falling away behind them. Now the goal would be to reach Anabiya before midnight. Fatima and Bolbol recovered their optimism and reviewed the necessities for their journey: bottles of mineral water, cigarettes, identity cards, and the little money they had left.

He died at the right time, Bolbol told himself. The body wouldn't rot as fast in this cold winter. They were fortunate he hadn't died in August, when flies swarm over and tear at the dead. Death is a solitary experience, of course, but nevertheless it lays heavy obligations on the living. There's a big difference between an old man who dies in his village, surrounded by family and close to the cemetery, and one who dies hundreds of kilometers away from them all. The living have a harder task ahead of them than the dead; no one wants to see their loved ones rot. They want them to look their best in death for that final memory that can never be erased. The last expression worn by a loved one necessarily comes to epitomize them. When the facial muscles of a suffering man slacken in the midst of his pain, his grief is what remains of him and he looks like nothing so much as a newborn child.

At the checkpoint outside the gate to Damascus, just before the highway, the soldier nodded inside the van and inquired what lay beneath the blanket. Bolbol said calmly, "My father's body." The soldier asked the question a second time, with a new edge in his voice, pointing to the heavy pile of blankets, and Bolbol reaffirmed his answer. The soldier motioned to Hussein to proceed into the GOODS TO DECLARE lane, where public-transport vehicles were lined up, and a different soldier, who was about twenty years old, was circling each one with a bomb detector. The soldier then left the checkpoint and went inside a one-room shed, previously a workshop and now used as an office as well as barracks for the checkpoint soldiers. After a few minutes, an officer marched toward the minibus, wrenched open the door, and ordered them to uncover the body. Bolbol lifted the blanket from his father's face. It was still fresh—his death still raw and tender. With studied callousness, the officer demanded the official documentation for the body, and

Fatima presented him with the death certificate signed by the director of the public hospital and the morgue official, together with their identity cards. He scrutinized the cards and then surprised them all by asking for the dead man's identity card as well. Bolbol almost started explaining to the man that all corpses share a single name—that they slip away from their histories and families in order to affirm their membership in one family alone, the family of the dead, and that no dead person can have any proof of identity beyond their death certificate—but Fatima slipped their father's identity card from her bag and offered it to the officer, who peered at the face of the body and then at the twenty-year-old picture on the card. In those days he had often laughed, their father; now, in death, his face was that of a stern, tough man. The officer took the identity cards and went back to his office. The three living occupants of the minibus exchanged glances and decided to wait in the bus without moving.

Hussein, in his place behind the wheel, was looking angrily at his watch and muttering inaudibly. One of the waiting truck drivers approached him and said plainly, "No goods can get through without the right *documents*." Hussein quickly got out of the minibus and went up to the makeshift office. He paid a bribe known as a goods-transit document, and their identity cards were returned. Feeling strangely victorious, he sped them all away from the checkpoint. Bolbol was thinking over the fact that his father was now a commodity like hookah coals, crates of tomatoes, sacks of onions. His ongoing silence discomfited Hussein, who announced that he had paid a thousand liras, and that they had to reach Anabiya before midnight.

For a moment Bolbol found himself wondering whether it might not be better to return to Damascus and arrange the burial in one of the graveyards there—although he knew this was absurd given how expensive graves were in Damascus. A good grave was so rare that people had begun advertising them in the classified ads, and they only had thirty-five thousand liras left among the three of them . . . Returning was out of the question; even if they had the money, how would they obtain official permission for a burial? Moreover, how could they convince the next shift of soldiers at the checkpoints they'd already passed that they had changed their minds? Or, indeed, that Abdel Latif had died in Damascus and not in a rebel town nearby?

After all, as a general rule, corpses don't much care about where they're buried. Just thinking about it frustrated Bolbol no end. It was a little past noon, he was tired, and he was fed up. Fatima lifted the blanket from her father's face, telling herself that a little fresh air, though cold, might do him good. She opened her window, even though the dead don't breathe and aren't likely to care whether the air is fresh or not. Bolbol told her to cover the body back up so the ice blocks packed tightly around it wouldn't melt, and Fatima complied without demur. Bolbol was now hoping they could all just ride in silence until they reached Anabiya. Their relatives would take care of the burial itself, and afterward he could escape from his family for the last time. He would go back to his nest and skulk in his room like a rat until his dream of moving to a faraway country was realized. There, in that distant land, he would inter himself in snow, and he would never complain about anything ever again. Right now, though, he couldn't keep from dwelling on the cramped and uncomfortable interior of the minibus, not to mention whatever surprises were bound to lie in store for them farther down the road, which he anticipated with dread. He couldn't think of anyone having successfully managed to transport a body all the way to Anabiya in three whole years.

Hussein felt uneasy at the silence, and since his memory didn't furnish him with a suitable pearl of wisdom, he snapped at Fatima to stop opening the window and then reminded his siblings spitefully that they wouldn't arrive at Anabiya before midnight, perhaps not even before dawn. Then he glanced at them in the rearview mirror, and the three of them exchanged looks of fear. All of their calculations had gone up in smoke; they'd already been delayed longer than they could have anticipated; there were few cars on the road, and the distant, blank wilderness—everything they could see, in fact—only made them more afraid.

At the beginning of the national highway, cars were turning onto a side road. Hussein asked a taxi driver if the highway was closed, and the man replied that there was a sniper up there, and he wasn't allowing anyone to pass. "He got *them* three hours ago," the driver added, pointing to four bodies lying on the road ahead: a man, a woman, a young man, and a girl. Bolbol considered the fact that they had chosen to die as they had lived: as a family. Hussein swerved the minibus onto the side road, following the other cars, and winding up in a series of narrow lanes. Somewhere nearby was being bombed, so close to them that they could see the bombs dropping out of the plane. Shrapnel was scattering around them. Hussein tried to block out everything but the road ahead. The last thing they needed was to find themselves pinned down in the middle of some burned-out olive grove.

A large number of cars were ahead of them. Doubtless one of the other drivers knew a safe route and was leading the charge. Bolbol wondered if they would wind up trapped where they were, but when he saw that all the other cars were now returning to the highway, hope was renewed. Hussein was already praising his own ingenuity in saving them from disaster; Bolbol was interested only in getting back to brooding about their dead father and wished Hussein would shut up. Bolbol noticed that the body was listing over; he tried to rearrange it to make it more stable. He considered tying it up somehow but wasn't prepared to have the debate this suggestion would open. Fatima reminded them of the sandwiches she'd brought for their long journey, and Hussein suggested that they pull over at the nearest rest stop when they began the approach to Homs. Bolbol hadn't eaten anything since the previous night. In his view, it was indecent to worry about food so soon after a parent's death.

Fatima was silent and put the sandwiches back in the plastic bag. Bolbol avoided looking at the right-hand side of the road. He was used to the sound of low-flying planes, the sounds of artillery and rocket launchers; for three years now there hadn't been a break in the noise. The bombardment of Qaboun and Jobar never stopped, and they could see traces of it on the buildings along the highway, but Bolbol wasn't interested—he remained indifferent to it all. Hussein drew their attention to the Qatifa checkpoint in the distance and said he would get right into the truck lane to save time. Bolbol made no objection and gave him some of his money. On the one hand, of course, Bolbol told himself, this was all a humiliating and ignominious experience, but then, on the other, it was difficult not to consider his father rather fortunate, given the thousands of corpses left out for birds of prey and other hungry scavengers . . . He tried not to dwell upon the four sniper victims who'd been left back on the highway, where no one dared to approach them, but his mind betrayed him, and he couldn't get the thought of them out of his head. All he wanted to do was lie down next to his father as he had done when he was a small boy, but the same fear that made him long for that comfort prevented him from sleeping so close to a dead man.

The long procession of trucks was exasperating; it would be hours before their turn came. Bolbol expected Hussein to try and expedite matters, but like him, Hussein was getting scared. He didn't dare to speak with the obviously irritable checkpoint guards. But Bolbol guessed that the agents manning the checkpoints were probably afraid, too; perhaps they would take pity on a dead man? He got out of the minibus and went over to the nearest officer and explained the situation with a concise and well-worded speech, but the officer didn't hear him; too many other people were talking to him as well, and Bolbol's voice was as weak and frightened as a wet baby bird in a moldy room. There was nothing for it: they were stuck in the line, with no way out. They were besieged by cars from all sides, and huge cement barriers prevented any vehicle from leaving its lane. On his way back to the minibus, Bolbol saw that Hussein was incensed at his behavior, as usual. He was telling Fatima that Bolbol was an idiot, a ditherer who had waited for them to reach the point of no return before lifting a finger to help, and then *still* failed to talk to the officer and convince him of their extraordinary circumstances. Fatima tried her best to alleviate the tension by telling both her brothers about her sister-in-law, who had been released from prison the previous week. The girl's face had turned yellow, she had lost half her body weight, and her head had been shaved to the bone. At night she raved deliriously. Fatima was sure she had been raped while she was inside. Hussein was ready to provide some pithy response, but Fatima went on, saying that the girl had scabies, too, so her family had been forced to isolate her in an old chicken coop on the roof, after all of which her fiancé dropped her and demanded compensation from her family.

The four bodies on the highway tarmac remained on Bolbol's mind, and now the story of Fatima's sister-in-law burrowed into him as well. It's often the case, in similar circumstances, on long journeys, that people will trade small talk and cheerful anecdotes to soften life's blows and distract from its cruelty: they'll talk about their children's achievements at school or the best season for making jam. But here in this minibus, such small talk as the siblings were able to muster did them absolutely no good; none of them could find any way to connect with the others. In ten years, the three of them hadn't been gathered in the same place for more than an hour or two during Eid, certainly not long enough for each to learn where life had brought the others. At first, when they'd left the hospital, they hadn't hidden their annoyance at being forced back together, but soon enough each sensed their common investment in avoiding any upsetting subjects. Here was a real opportunity to talk about whether they could possibly be a family again—but Hussein didn't care, Bolbol actively opposed it, and Fatima was too busy trying to play the role of the noble sister reuniting her family after the death of a parent. It was a role she had heard a lot about: it was something like her natural inheritance. The older brother inherits the role of the father, and the sister by necessity inherits the mother's role; but in this case it required a strength that Fatima, who'd grown old, didn't possess. She had become a mother, yes, but not like her own. She had given up her dreams of wealth, making do with a lot of complaining and occasionally hiding away a little money from her and her husband's salaries in a bank account no one knew about. She had become a miser on account of her humble income, collecting any castoffs from her childhood home and accepting charity from her in-laws. Her middling intelligence left her looking forever forlorn. All that remained to her now was the hope that either her son or her daughter would somehow compensate her for her lost dreams, so she might finally take revenge on the world for the loss of the pride she'd been famed for when she was a girl, convinced that she was striding purposefully toward a life of brilliance and happiness.

Fatima was nearly forty now, and the traces of her lost pride were still visible on her face. Everyone who loses their pride becomes a miser of a sort; their self-importance increases, their eyes die out, and their resentments accumulate. They incline to gossip and tell stories about all the heroic things that didn't happen in the life they never lived. Fatima, too, passed through all these stages and, in the end, surrendered. She focused on her son (who had entered a dentistry school) and her daughter. The latter was still only fourteen, but Fatima liked it when people said that they resembled each other, droning automatically, "What a pretty girl!" Fatima had prepared her children for a very different life and often repeated to them the story of her first marriage to a great businessman. In reality, he had been nothing more than a small-time fixer who liked running with the big shots. He facilitated their dealings with government agencies and carried out their dirty work, such as watching their wives whenever business took them abroad or accompanying their underage daughters on shopping trips to Beirut.

Fatima would sometimes recall the day they met. On that day, Fatima had been waiting for the bus that would take her to a teacher-training institute in Mezzeh. It was pouring rain, and the bus stop was crowded, and she accepted Mamdouh's invitation to give her a lift in all innocence. She thought he was a friend of her brother's and got into his car without more than an instant of hesitation. She was astonished when he told her that he was always seeing her at the bus stop and that he liked her. He added that he was a student of her father's at the high school. She accepted it, all of it, as quite normal: he liked her, and it wouldn't stop there. She secretly believed that most young men felt the same way about her and that this one just happened to be the only man with the courage to say so. Like all her classmates, she had composed many an imaginary tale about being pursued by lovers, and his presence in her life satisfied this vanity in front of her classmates. She intended them all to see it when her suitor drove her to the institute every morning, and she took her sweet time getting out of the car, speaking to him as if issuing orders while he nodded deferentially. Even though she had liked him from the first instant, she wouldn't surrender so easily; she dealt with him quite loftily and was coy about her feelings. Deep down, she held herself in high regard, and Mamdouh patiently professed himself delighted to obey her every whim. He was as much attracted to her illusions about him as to her, since she supposed him to be an exceptional person; she spoke about their future in an outlandish manner, full of unrealistic enthusiasm and optimism, and Mamdouh was delighted with it all. She liked his stylishness and his little gifts, which were limited to bottles of perfume, Italian shoes, and jeans, all ersatz but made to look like they came from grand shops in Damascus. She was absolutely entranced by his seductive words about love and the happy family they would be devoted to building.

It was a quiet sort of love story. Fatima convinced herself that even if Mamdouh wasn't rich *now*, a man with his connections, with such fine manners and so much wisdom about life, would doubtless get rich by and by, and so she married him despite her father's objections. Her father said it was impossible that such a proud girl should marry a man indistinguishable from any other, a man he described as "mercury," and moreover one who had no demonstrable moral values or virtues to prevent him from becoming a pimp. Fatima defended Mamdouh calmly, and her father eventually surrendered, although he foresaw her future misery, and the thought of it hurt him deeply.

Mamdouh tried to adapt to married life, but it turned out that his patience for his wife's grandiose delusions—about her beauty, her family's influence, her general estimation of herself—was limited. It was all exaggeration: she was just an ordinary, unremarkable girl. She persisted in believing that her looks and natural elegance were renowned, that everything she did could be described only as perfection, while in reality she fell far short of her ideal. From the very first month, Mamdouh knew the marriage was a mistake; he discovered that Fatima's misapprehensions—which he had assumed were just words, and words that would soon be forgotten at that—were for Fatima indisputable facts in which she had absolute faith. And despite her genuine attraction to Mamdouh, particularly in the early days of their marriage, when she was still working all her long-endured sexual frustration out of her system— frustration left over from those lonely years when other men had found her beauty too imposing to ever approach her—she was soon terribly bored. She put up with it and tried to give everyone the impression that they were happy together nonetheless. Her self-confidence and pride made her believe she was capable of remolding her husband. His supposed weakness and the supposed power (largely imaginary) she held over Mamdouh served to satisfy her ego, but she no longer felt so certain of controlling him as she had before their marriage. All her attempts to impose a different regimen on his life were unsuccessful. Their relationship began to lose all savor, and it didn't last the year. To Mamdouh, Fatima was just a short, failed experiment in matrimony. His ardor was slaked, and he could no longer stand to live with this remote and fatuous woman, whose family had allowed her to treat her fantasies as fact. Reflecting on his dilemma, he decided to escape before Fatima became a mother and his own folly also became a fact from which he could never be free. He told her he was going abroad to make his fortune and gave her the option of a divorce or waiting until he returned from Greece, adding that it was possible he might never come back.

After the divorce, her father said bitterly, "She married for the sake of some takeout from Broasted Express and the chance of sitting with some big shots in their fancy ballrooms." These big shots regarded Fatima as the wife of a servant, nothing more, but their good-natured acceptance of her presence among them led her to believe she could count herself as their friend, with the right to participate in all their private affairs. She would ask the wife of a Japanese company's local agent about the best slimming club in Damascus and wait gravely for a reply, or she would confess to the wife of a French oil company agent that she didn't want to have a child for a few more years so that she could keep her stomach from sagging for as long as possible. The following day, back in the school where she was now a teacher, she would yawn in the staff room and grumble nonchalantly about her husband's never-ending late nights with his friends and business associates. The aura of prestige always contains a little foolishness, and Fatima greatly enjoyed playing the fool, however unwittingly, especially when she saw the prospect of credulity in her colleagues' eyes.

After Mamdouh's departure, Fatima returned to her old room in the family home, reeling with dented pride, in utter disbelief that everything was over and that her total value had been reduced to six suitcases crammed with worn-out clothes and shoes, a collection of fake perfume bottles, and the balance of her dowry of two hundred thousand liras, which Mamdouh had paid after both parties signed the divorce contract.

That day, Bolbol had sat next to his father in his capacity as the elder brother, by no means enjoying this distinction. His father's concealed rage kept him silent for a long time; this insult to the dignity he had maintained all his life had cut him deeply, and Bolbol sympathized with this respectable man who had been forced, because of his idiotic daughter, to shake hands with a student he considered worthless. Their father settled the matter swiftly, opened the door, and asked Mamdouh to leave. That night was the first time Bolbol truly realized that his father would die one day. Abdel Latif had gone into his room, closed the door, and wouldn't speak to anyone for days. Afterward, as he did whenever he felt weak, he went to Anabiya, where he was content to walk through the meadows and respond to invitations from childhood friends to play cards and reminisce a little. After he returned from these visits, his confidence and sense of self were restored.

When it was their turn at the checkpoint, the agent on duty told Hussein that the Mukhabarat would have to check their identity cards while he examined the corpse. Bolbol sincerely wished that his father had indeed died on that day long ago, when it would have been so easy to carry out his request that he be buried with his sister. Kindhearted neighbors would have come by to condole with them as they had done when his mother died. On that occasion, a delegation of four men had accompanied the family to the graveyard, which was four hundred kilometers from the village, and one of them even hosted an additional ʿaza for the departed on their return. The neighbors prepared a generous feast for the mourners, grateful that Ustadh Abdel Latif al-Salim had allowed them to share his grief.

Bolbol saw Hussein coming back, escorted by an agent waving his gun and gesturing to the rest of the family to get out of the van. Hussein stood next to Bolbol and whispered, "They're going to arrest the body." Bolbol assumed there must have been some mistake, but no, when the agent led them to a tiled, windowless room, opened the door, and pushed them roughly inside, he understood that things were serious. It was true: they had placed the corpse under arrest. Their father had been wanted by more than one branch of the Mukhabarat for more than two years now.

The cell was crowded with more than twenty people of different ages. One of them, a woman of about seventy, told Fatima without being asked that she was being held hostage in her son's stead, who had deserted from the army last year. Another, a young man of around twenty, missing a hand, told them that the Mukhabarat suspected him of having lost his hand fighting as an insurgent, and not in a car accident years before. He added that he and the two friends he was sitting with there in the improvised holding cell had been on their way to catch a boat from Turkey to Greece, intending to travel from there to Sweden. He'd never believed their journey would be as simple as that, particularly as their lives were bound to their identity cards, which showed their place of residence as Baba Amr, in the city of Homs. Like all young men from Baba Amr, one of the first places where revolution broke out and which was punished by merciless bombardment as a result, they had gotten accustomed to being stopped at every checkpoint. Meanwhile, other prisoners were snoring loudly or staring silently into the shadowy corners of the cell, their expressions making plain their sense of degradation. They had been here for some time, and bruises from beatings could be seen on their faces. One of them was wearing pants stained with clotted blood; his head was wrapped in his shirt. Bolbol tried to will himself to look at these people; no one knew what would happen to them once they were transferred to whichever branch of the Mukhabarat wanted them. He looked at Fatima, still listening to that old woman who wouldn't stop chattering about her son, saying that it didn't matter anymore if she died, and she was glad he'd deserted. Bolbol told himself that no doubt Fatima would now tell the old woman about her sister-in-law's rape and her fiancé's desertion; this last detail had stimulated Fatima's appetite for gossip.

From his position in the corner, tucked away as much as possible, Bolbol could see the faces in the shadows of the room: dark, afraid, and sad. The detainees murmured to one another in voices like the droning of an old bee, monotonous and incessant. It was impossible to say what would happen to any of them. No one could enter a place like this and know what was in store for them. So many people had disappeared in the previous four years, it was no longer even shocking; there were tens of thousands whose fates were unknown. Hussein asked Fatima to say that she was divorced from Mamdouh but not to mention her remarriage, believing that her first husband's name and regime connections might improve the siblings' standing with their jailers. Fatima nodded without asking why this mattered. She knew how much he liked giving commands, and she generally liked to obey him. Taking up their old roles made them feel less afraid, and they would go through these motions as often during their journey as they had—without ever understanding why—during their childhood.

The floor of the cell was cold, and the loud, nonstop conversation of the Mukhabarat agents came in through the one small window. Bolbol remained aloof from the detainees, careful not to say a word, careful not to get himself in trouble. He asked no questions and allowed no one to question him and avoided so much as feeling sympathy when he heard stories that ought to have aroused immeasurable rage and sadness. He could almost have fallen asleep were it not for the clanging of the huge iron door as it opened every now and again. His memory summoned up the tales he had heard of the horrendous tortures endured by detainees in just such situations. The facts related by those fortunate enough to be released from cells like these were discussed and circulated everywhere, too terrifying to be believed. In his heart he knew that he would never be able to endure torn-out fingernails or electrocution or suffocating indefinitely in a congested cell or being forced to walk over rotting corpses. Probably he would just die after his first session. He closed his eyes, oddly reassured by this. He, at least, would leave behind a corpse with no last will or request; he didn't even care if his body was reduced to ashes or left for the dogs to gnaw. When the time came, he would be capable of lying next to his father without fear. This thought gave him the courage he needed, without having to boast of any real or imaginary exploits.

The next agent to open the door asked for one of the relatives of the corpse in the minibus to please step forward. Hussein ignored him, still absorbed in a long conversation about car tires with the three young men who had been on their way to Sweden. His animated features communicated his deep satisfaction as a torrent of aphorisms flowed from his tongue with an eloquence wholly unsuited to this environment. Bolbol was forced to get up when the soldier beckoned him to follow.

He was brought to an officer who couldn't have been more

than thirty. All of the family's documents were in his hands: their identity cards and the death certificate signed in accordance with the proper regulations. The officer asked Bolbol for details of every single family member and friend of his father. He said he would transfer them to the main facility for questioning and detain the body, likewise in accordance with the proper regulations. Though the officer's cool tone left little hope, Bolbol pleaded with him to be allowed to continue with their journey, adding that he himself supported the current regime—he and his father had been estranged!—and going on to say that he had lived in the suburb of M, where a mix of religions was found, for more than twenty years. Bolbol heaped curses on his father for the benefit of the officer, who once again turned over the papers in his hands and looked at them contemptuously. The short silence that followed these pleas allowed Bolbol to hope that the officer wasn't serious about handing the family over to the Mukhabarat . . . but he didn't know how he could plead for mercy for his father's body.

The officer explained that according to their records, Bolbol's father was still alive and still wanted. It didn't matter if he had in the meantime turned into a cadaver. Then he added that his commanding officer would settle the matter in the end and asked Bolbol to go through to the other room to fill in and sign this and that form. Bolbol was dripping with sweat. They really were going to take the body. Yet another agent went into the holding cell and took the minibus keys from Hussein. He drove it to a nearby garage and locked it, notifying the guard that it wasn't to be taken off the premises without the express permission of the officer in charge.

This same agent came back and led Bolbol into the next room and said that it wasn't the first time this had happened. Another corpse had been arrested the previous month and sent under armed escort to Tishreen Military Hospital, where a committee had had to look into the matter and sign off on the body's status. The corpse wasn't surrendered to its family until all the appropriate procedures had been followed, which the agent then took it upon himself to explain at length. First, they entailed going to the civil-records office and updating the deceased's status, then going to the central registry and issuing a cable that would suspend the outstanding warrant. The body would be kept in custody until being transferred to the military hospital for examination, where the death of the wanted man would be confirmed and the legal procedures to permanently cancel the search warrant completed. The agent couldn't seem to make up his mind from one sentence to the next as to whether the state regarded a person as being merely a collection of documents or rather an entity of flesh, blood, and soul. Bolbol nodded desperately and asked the agent to go into more detail, but eventually he stopped talking and ordered his prisoner to go ahead and fill out the form.

Bolbol felt the pressure of the silent agent's observation as he wrote in the required details about his family members and the members of their extended families and then surrendered the form. Gathering his courage, he offered a bribe to the agent who had explained the procedures to him, referring to it demurely as a "goods-transit document." The agent gave him a sardonic glance, but they agreed on twenty thousand liras—if the body was released. The agent took Bolbol back to the holding cell and wished him luck, saying that he hoped the commanding officer would settle the matter swiftly, and adding that they would keep the family at the checkpoint till the arrival of the cable that would determine their fate.

Time passed slowly; the prisoners were all ensnared in their various conversations, which Bolbol resolved to ignore. He was thinking of the labyrinth they would be lost in if the Mukhabarat really decided to transfer the body to the military hospital. His fear increased every time he thought of the possibility that a person might be nothing more than a collection of papers. He heard the old woman describing the destruction of Homs to Fatima, adding that she had been arrested three times since the revolution—she pronounced the word openly and without fear—but that this was the first time she'd ever been held as a hostage. Bolbol wasn't surprised at the old woman's mettle; she reminded him of his father and his father's friends, in whose hearts fear had seemingly died forever. But he was surprised at Fatima's zeal in narrating the tale of her sister-in-law, which she naturally launched into as soon as she was given an opportunity. She asked the old woman if it was true that the secret police raped women being detained, and the woman laughed and murmured, "Men too," adding that a thousand years would pass before this outrage would be forgotten.

Whenever the door opened, an agent would throw a new prisoner inside. The cell was getting more and more intolerably crowded, but everyone knew that they wouldn't be there long; they couldn't be kept there all night, otherwise their jailers would already have separated the men from the women. Bolbol wondered whether there might not be a real prison in the nearby complex, something older and more permanent than this temporary setup, but he halted that train of thought immediately, telling himself that holding cells were one commodity still more than plentiful in his country. The door opened again: a mother and her two children came in. She wasn't kept waiting long. She sat by the old woman and Fatima and told them that she didn't know what she was being accused of; she had been on her way to Beirut, where her husband worked in construction, and they had ordered her to get off the bus she had boarded at Deir Azzour. A few minutes later, the woman said that she had six brothers in the Free Army, and now they had been forced to fight alongside a battalion of Islamic extremists in al-Mayadin, since their own funding had been cut off and their supplies had run out. She added that many Free Army troops had defected to the Islamist side because they supposedly had more money. The woman said all this in a loud voice; Bolbol kept a safe distance as he observed her.

Bolbol got up when he saw Hussein had at last run out of steam. He wanted to make the peril of their enforced idleness clear, to explain the labyrinth he had foreseen them all entering, had foreseen overwhelming them, but he changed his mind when he saw that his brother, even half asleep, was still blathering about tires. Bolbol went up to the cell door instead and caught the eye of the agent he'd spoken with earlier, miming that he wanted another word. The agent opened the cell door, and Bolbol reminded him of their agreement; the agent promised that everything would be all right if they raised the sum from twenty to thirty thousand. Bolbol said this was fine, but explained that they weren't from a well-off family and that this sum was all they had in the world. The agent returned Bolbol to the cell and asked him to stay close to the door.

Bolbol sat next to Hussein and explained everything to him. Hussein was taken aback; he'd secretly been hoping that the body's being impounded by the police might actually prove the best possible outcome—saving the family from who knew what dangers might still await them on their trip. Bolbol steeled himself to deliver the news that they could of course still be detained as hostages . . . Hussein scratched his head and found himself let down by his memory once again; no anecdote or saying seemed entirely germane to their situation. He pushed the question to one side and said that if the Mukhabarat had taken the corpse into custody, they would have to dispose of it themselves. They could burn it or sell the organs or throw it into a mass grave—what would the dead person care, after all? Bolbol was astonished. He felt his brother's burgeoning fear deeply, not to mention Hussein's everpresent wish to take revenge on their father one way or another. In Bolbol's opinion, though, contrary to Hussein's, losing the body to the security forces would plunge the family into a mire from which they'd never be able to extricate themselves—a trap in which details would get so tangled they would never figure out what had happened to them. Hussein agreed to leave Bolbol to sort everything out, and although Bolbol felt entirely impotent, he was less afraid at this moment than at any other time in his life.

An hour later, the same agent opened the door and pushed a new prisoner inside. Bolbol reminded him of their situation and their agreement, and the agent asked him to come outside. The money changed hands discreetly, after which the agent returned to the cell and pointed at Hussein and Fatima and told them to stand up and leave at once. He reminded them that they still needed to send the death certificate to the civil-records office and make sure their father was struck off the list of wanted criminals.

A few minutes later, they were waiting outside the officer's room. The agent who had pocketed their money opened the door for them and disappeared, leaving them to his superior, who proceeded to address them at length on the latest news of their case. He informed the family that his commanding officer had asked him to confirm the death of the criminal personally, and thereby close the file and allow his family to bury him. All three siblings stood in front of him politely and attentively as he spoke; they praised the kind heart of the commander, who had looked on their situation with a sympathetic eye and refrained from requiring that the body be sent to a medical committee to verify what was obviously true. After refusing to provide them with an official document verifying that the warrant for their father had been canceled, which would have prevented other checkpoints from holding and questioning them yet again, the officer concluded his short speech and said that their way would be clear after this checkpoint; their problems would lie with the checkpoints set up by the terrorists nearer to Aleppo. The officer said the word "terrorists" most emphatically, then indicated with a brief wave of his hand that they should leave before he changed his mind, or anyway before a telegram arrived demanding that the corpse be taken back into custody. In such a case, there would be no alternative but to obey orders. One gesture from the commander, he repeated, and their lives would once again be turned into a living hell.

It wasn't the first time they had been made to stand attentively in front of such exhortations, but it was certainly the first time they'd been so close to sliding into the labyrinth. Bolbol had by no means been confident of the outcome of all his negotiations, so he was overjoyed when the minibus was allowed to leave the checkpoint, and the whole complex soon lay some distance behind them. He felt he'd been very close to the ultimate moment—the moment he had avoided for four years. He had felt this same giddiness before, whenever he escaped arrest for a crime he hadn't committed. On those occasions, his identity card with its incriminating birthplace had been the principal problem; now, the body of his father, the wanted man, had almost drowned them all.

Evening brought back all their fear and confusion, however.

Hussein was offended now that Bolbol had struck the deal alone. He considered it irresponsible for an amateur like him to have handled a case as grave as theirs—it ought to have called for his own expert negotiation and people-reading skills. He managed not to complain about it and made do with stating that they had to think of where they would spend the night, adding a casual comment that thirty thousand liras was pretty steep just to ensure safe conduct for a shipment of smuggled goods. Bolbol was afraid that Hussein would conclude by saying that their father wasn't worth this sum when he was alive, so how could he be worth it dead? Really the price should have dropped by at least three quarters, as with selling used shoes.

Hussein didn't say it—but neither could he keep quiet. In fact, he soon suggested that they toss the body out on the roadside, asking his brother and sister how confident they were that they would pass other checkpoints without trouble. They would be right back where they started if the next checkpoint agents discovered that their father was a wanted man. He added that the dogs were eating plenty of bodies nowadays, so what difference did it make? Why didn't they just leave it or bury it anywhere and go back to Damascus?

Bolbol could tell that Hussein wasn't joking this time; he wanted an answer, wanted his brother and sister to make a decision. Bolbol wanted to ignore him, but suddenly a great strength welled up inside him, and he declared he wouldn't abandon his father's body before his last wish was carried out. Fatima agreed and asked Hussein to speed up, even though it would be impossible for them to arrive at Anabiya that night in any case. The highway came to an end a few kilometers before Homs, and they would have to use the side roads, which were dangerous at night; no rational being would even consider traveling them in the company of a dead man.

Whenever Bolbol saw trucks crossing checkpoints with ease, he wished his father's body would turn into a sack of cumin; it was hard to see any downside to such a transformation—in fact, reaching a state of mutual understanding with a sack of cumin would be easier and far less dangerous. He deeply regretted promising his father to do as he'd asked. Forget about changing Abdel Latif into a sack of cumin—Bolbol would have been content to see himself transformed into a man with a little less sympathy.

The night before, he had sat on the bed next to his father while Abdel Latif told him in a feeble voice that his death was very near. Bolbol tried to divert his father's attention from these forebodings and thought briefly that his father was just having a nightmare, thanks to the death all around and the bombings that hadn't been silent for three years—that Abdel Latif was entering one of his states of delirium, which had become more and more frequent in the past month. Of course, you didn't have to be sick to have the same problems. Everyone suffered from insomnia and interrupted sleep these days, from panic attacks and nervous breakdowns; everyone spent entire nights discussing sleep aids, such as chamomile flowers brewed with rosemary, milk mixed with crushed garlic, or Faustan-brand sleeping pills; Bolbol, too, liked to talk over the recipes he'd tried, or to discuss with his colleagues how best to cover their windows with plastic wrap so that the glass wouldn't become shrapnel when it shattered. Recipes and helpful hints were also frequent topics of discussion for the people stuck at checkpoints for hours in the scorching afternoons and under the pouring rain. Taking naps was good; it helped the dreary evenings pass a little more quickly. Small things like that could cheer people up . . . or, alternatively, could destroy their lives and drive them out into the unknown, as in the case of this corpse, which had begun to turn rotten. When they left the hospital, they hadn't wondered what would happen to them. All three were too busy calculating how long it had been since they had last spoken to one another. Their throats were clogged with words that would rust and waste away if they weren't finally let out. Fatima at least wanted to regain some tenderness in her relationships with her brothers, but Bolbol had no desire to concede a thing to his siblings. Certainly there had been times when he wanted to return to that old familial harmony, but usually he felt that there was simply too much distance between them now. Getting away from them was the only positive thing he'd accomplished in the last ten years, he thought sometimes. And if they were honest, his sister and brother felt the same way, painful though it would be for anyone to admit—all believed that they had already done more than their duty for the family. Now it was time to consider their own lives.

Yes, the previous night, their father had felt keenly that he was dying. He had done everything he wanted to do in this life and had said everything he needed to say during his stay with Bolbol. But despite the illness, Bolbol hadn't believed his father would really die. It wasn't credible that anyone could still die of natural causes in this day and age. Even his neighbor Um Elias had been murdered, though she was in her eighties. A young relative and his friends conspired to break into her house and force open her strongbox, which everyone said contained millions of liras and several kilograms of gold. She put up a fight and recognized them, so they killed her. The police were even forced to follow it up and do a little actual police work so the killing wouldn't be recorded as a sectarian crime. That would have sent the Christian inhabitants of the quarter into a panic.

Not that the neighbors were too upset about old Um Elias, who had made a living selling miserly amounts of watered-down alcohol to them, but nevertheless they came as a body and spat at the young man in question, barely twenty years old, as he was forced into a police car. The police took him to the apartment in Rukneddine where he'd hidden the stolen goods in a well next to the graveyard. His two accomplices lived in the same building, and they didn't try to flee but surrendered and confessed in full. The following morning the three criminals were quietly brought before an examining magistrate. He was frustrated, as the crime of murder no longer called for such caution and care, and the criminals' easy confession increased his irritation. They would all find a way to avoid prison anyhow, the easiest route being to accept a position among the murderers of the regime militias, though there was always the chance that the resistance might storm the prison, knock down the walls, and destroy their files regardless.

In recent months, when people died, no one bothered asking after the hows and the whys. They already knew the answers all too well: bombings, torture during detention, kidnappings, a sniper's bullet, a battle. As for dying of grief, for example, or being let down by your body, deaths like that were rare—and no one lamented a death that didn't have any outrage attached to it.

Before Bolbol and his siblings left Damascus, he had called his office and requested a leave of absence. He received the indifferent condolences of his colleagues over the phone and asked that no one take the trouble of condoling with him in person, or indeed trouble themselves with helping him arrange the burial. He was still feeling the same deeply rooted fury as when the young doctor on duty told him his father's heart had stopped. If his father had died three months earlier, when he was still in the village of S, then everything would have been easy. The cemeteries there were large and plentiful, and any one of the people still living in the town could have buried him with all the consideration due to the great and illustrious *ustadh*, their comrade in revolution from its first day to his last. They would have considered him a martyr. Bolbol's only responsibility would have been to hear about it—and then pass along word to Hussein and Fatima and spread the news by calling their few relatives still in Anabiya, some of whom would certainly have supported Bolbol to carry out his duty of looking mournful and organizing a small ʿaza for a few close friends. But that body lying on its hospital bed, and the glances of the on-call doctor— they only made Bolbol feel trapped. Death had become hard work. Just as hard as living, in Bolbol's view.

The doctor had instructed the orderlies to cover Abdel Latif's face and carry him to the morgue, and then asked Bolbol to sign for the body and get it off the premises before the following afternoon. If not, they would be forced to deal with it themselves. Priority in the overcrowded hospital morgue was given to the bodies of soldiers.

When he used to think about it, Bolbol hadn't reckoned on his father's death being such a disaster for him. He had half hoped that if Abdel Latif needed to die nearby, it would be somewhere closed off by a siege or while Bolbol was traveling far away. In such a case, he would have been absolved from the duty of arranging everything, and responsibility for his father's last wish would have had to be shouldered by Hussein, who wouldn't have hesitated to ignore it.

One night, three days before Abdel Latif died, Bolbol took his father to the hospital after his pains grew worse. It was lucky they stumbled across a taxi by the all-night *fuul* restaurant. Finding a driver willing to cross the city from east to west, not to mention finding a vacant bed in the public hospital, was such a stroke of luck that God should have received their utmost thanks—and Bolbol really did do his best to feel grateful. He gave the taxi driver the fare he had requested plus a tip for helping his father onto a stretcher; he insisted on staying with Bolbol until he was assured that Abdel Latif wouldn't get abandoned by the hospital staff in some corridor. Then again, the driver, too, probably preferred to be in the hospital than on the dangerous streets at night. Bolbol didn't ask him why he didn't go home; he was afraid of the answer. On an earlier occasion, trying to make small talk in a taxi, he had been unwise enough to ask the driver when his shift was over and he could go home, but the driver had sneered and described his house in Zamalka in detail, including the fact that it had been bombed and his wife lay dead beneath the rubble. In the end he had asked Bolbol, "So what home do you mean, sir?"

For months, Bolbol had avoided talking to anyone he didn't know or even leaving the house. Going outside was hard work. He was content to travel back and forth from work and read state newspapers ostentatiously on the bus. On his days off, he watched black-and-white Egyptian films on cable and grieved for this golden bygone era. He didn't know why he put himself through this, but at least this was a pastime that no one could possibly find suspicious; everyone was mourning for the beautiful days that they'd lost. Longer holidays such as Eid he spent making different types of pickles. He liked the new strategies he'd developed in order to keep himself sane, even though they were all strictly short-term arrangements. He didn't dare acknowledge that his life was a collection of trivial acts that would sooner or later have to come to an end.

One day, his isolation was punctured. One of his father's neighbors' sons—an engineering student turned combatant in the Free Syrian Army—called Bolbol and informed him that his father's health made it very difficult for him to remain in the besieged village. Bolbol couldn't bring himself to say anything in reply—not out of shock from hearing about his father's deterioration, but from fear of being arrested for speaking to a person who lived in S. The caller didn't have a lot of time and said that they had been fortunate enough to manage to smuggle the *ustadh* out to the abandoned gas station at the edge of the village. He asked Bolbol to arrive at six o'clock that evening to take him away.

The call had come at three in the afternoon. Bolbol couldn't chance saying a word to this person calling from an unknown number. What if the line was tapped? He was absolutely certain that the regime monitored every word coming out of the village. He had to think of a way out of this terrible mistake. Suddenly one of his rare bursts of self-assurance led him to decide to resolve the matter. He thought he would call Hussein. His brother should help in a situation like this. He dialed Hussein's number and was overcome with frustration when he heard that phone service had been temporarily interrupted. There was still time, though. Hussein would probably get back to him when he saw the missed call. Bolbol sat in a neighborhood restaurant in Saruja and asked for beans and rice. He contemplated what he was about to do to himself: his father was going to come and live with him in his small house. Well, maybe his father wouldn't be able to endure being in a district loyal to the regime.

Bolbol had worked hard to gain the trust of his neighborhood.

The details on his identity card marked him out for suspicion; for four years now, similar details had spelled catastrophe for many others. Thousands of people disappeared without a trace, simply for being born in areas controlled by the opposition, just as many regime supporters had disappeared in those same areas. Kidnappings, ransoms, and random arrests were widespread and tit-for-tat responses meant they only escalated in frequency. People's movements were tightly controlled. Any error could be very costly.

Bolbol minimized his time in public. To get to work he took the special bus for public employees, and to get home in the evening he took the same route back—like so many others whose identity cards and official documents happened to list the names of various now burned-out towns under "Birthplace." He abandoned his few remaining old habits, such as visiting a coffeehouse every Friday, or loafing around Bab Tuma. He cut short any burgeoning friendships with his colleagues; all they ever did together was repeat the same conversations about rising prices anyway . . . and by the time they started furtively discussing indications that they had gleaned which pointed to recent regime losses, using code words familiar to opposition sympathizers, Bolbol had already taken to ignoring them. He didn't want to venture so much as an ambiguous comment—he simply acted as if he hadn't heard anything at all and then returned to the subject of his pickling projects, grumbling about the rising price of eggplant.

Three months before the long drive to Anabiya, there was a knock on Bolbol's door at dawn. Three young men came in, boys from the neighborhood, all armed, accompanied by a local official who treated Bolbol with something like contempt. They ignored all his questions and overturned everything in the house. Not even the big portrait of the president in the middle of the living room won him any favor. Bolbol was offended, but kept quiet. He'd already scoured his home of everything that might have caused him harm in this situation: purging each and every suspicious belonging and even canceling all the television channels that regime supporters considered "biased," such as Al Jazeera and Al Arabiya, and filling his "Favorites" list with pro-regime channels: first came Al Manar and Al Mayadeen (the satellite channels run by Hezbollah), followed by Alalam from Iran, the Syrian News Channel, and then various other innocuous choices, like National Geographic, some food channels, and so forth. He'd gone over every inch of the place dozens of times to confirm to himself that the house was "clean." He only wished he could change his ID number and his place of birth. Anyway, the soldiers searched the house carefully and left without apology, letting Bolbol drown in the chaos of his scattered possessions. They cursed him and his hometown, as usual, but Bolbol did his best to ignore it; he told himself they were just goading him into reacting so they had an excuse to kill him. Of course, if they shot him, his blood would be spilled for nothing. Defending himself against some mild abuse would hardly make him a martyr. When they were well and truly gone, he congratulated himself on successfully passing this thousandth security check. After this he gradually gained the qualified approval of his poverty-stricken neighbors, who likewise used to curse his birthplace loudly whenever he walked down the street. He had chosen to live in this poor neighborhood after his divorce from Hiyam; she had made it a condition that he leave all their furniture with her to pay off the balance of her dowry and in exchange for her raising their only son—another Abdel Latif. The boy had been named after his grandfather, as though to prove that Bolbol still had strong links to his family, in the absence of any other evidence.

Really, all of Bolbol's behavior was an imitation of his father's—an attempt to live longer in his shadow. That respected gentleman, weighted with idealism, lived in the past, a remnant of some dreamlike former age. His vocabulary and habits dated back to a different world and would not conform to standards of the present day. Bolbol's father boasted of belonging to an era of "the greatest values and elegance," as he called the sixties, adding that it had been quite lovely to boot. Bolbol often caught himself using the same flowery old words as his father. And he still remembered his father's hysterical reaction when Hussein dismissed his precious 1960s as just a mirage—announcing that everything people said about those days was a lie that should finally be put to rest, and that those years were in fact the era of all the Muslim world's defeats. His father had been furious for the rest of the day. That was probably the first time any member of the family had dared to contradict him or sully his sacrosanct memories.

As Abdel Latif had aged, he only became more attached to those memories of his youth, down to the tiniest details: a certain way of shining his shoes, a particularly elegant necktie, a way of speaking concisely and listening respectfully, making witty comments and telling anecdotes whenever his old friends were gathered. It was important to him to be charming, to hold a constructive and enjoyable salon. He considered his duties sacred, and the town of S never saw a funeral in which he wasn't a participant. He remembered all his friends' birthdays and other special occasions and shared the few supplies he was able to see brought in from Anabiya. According to his students, he was a strange man, though likewise a respected inhabitant of their town for more than forty years, who had arrived to teach in the school and soon became one of them. They originally called him the Anabiyan, in reference to his hometown, but everyone forgot this nickname with the passage of time, and he became, simply, Ustadh Abdel Latif.

Bolbol couldn't get through to Hussein. He felt cold to his bones. There was no choice but to go alone to pick up his father. The sheer density of the checkpoints between him and the rendezvous point meant the length of the journey was out of his control, but he still managed to arrive at the appointed time. When he saw his father leaning on the wall of the abandoned gas station, Bolbol felt empty inside. His father was somewhat dazed and had lost a lot of weight; his face was haggard, his breath was foul, and it was clear that he hadn't eaten for some days. Even so, he was clean-shaven, wore a tie, and his clothes were spotless.

Abdel Latif smiled when he saw Bolbol coming toward him. Bolbol squeezed his father's hand. A group of armed young men appeared from nowhere, some of whom Bolbol recognized, and they all raised their hands in farewell to their comrade as they passed. Abdel Latif refused to lie down in the back seat of the taxi. Bolbol asked his father not to talk to the driver; he might be an informer, and Bolbol knew the sorts of things his father was likely to say—open praise for the people of his rebel town and curses for the regime. Bolbol didn't say a word, praying that everything would work out. He asked Abdel Latif what medicines he needed, but his father just shook his head and proceeded to glower at every checkpoint soldier with overt resentment.

When they got home, Bolbol laid him down on the bed and went out to find a doctor. He reflected that the doctors of this neighborhood might also be informers who would consider Abdel Latif a terrorist if they knew where he'd been these last few years—stubbornly clinging on inside that besieged village. But there were rumors about a back-street doctor named Nizar, who had been thrown in jail at the beginning of the revolution, and who'd had some public clashes with the rest of the neighborhood when he refused to give up his home in it. After tracking him down, Bolbol more or less explained the situation, and the doctor—who turned out to be a kind and conscientious young man—accompanied Bolbol to his house as soon as he was finished with one more consultation. On the way, Bolbol told him that they were originally from the town of S, a veiled reference to where their sympathies lay. The doctor caught it at once, and the name of the town was all it took to rouse the young doctor's fervent respect.

The doctor was assiduous in his care. Abdel Latif always used to say that the children of the revolution were everywhere, which was why they would, in the end, prevail. The doctor was surprised to find a portrait of the president hanging in the living room but made no comment about it on that first visit. The next day, Bolbol explained his position in the neighborhood, implying that he himself was a clandestine revolutionary. The doctor didn't care for this obvious dissimulation, considering Bolbol's tack to be little better than collaboration with the regime, but he well understood Bolbol's anxiety and felt reassured as to his basic good nature when Bolbol gave him a couple of jars of pickled cucumbers and peppers. The doctor brought over various drugs free of charge and became a firm friend of Abdel Latif. He visited every day, and the two would whisper together. Their eyes would gleam when Bolbol's father told his doctor friend stories of life inside the siege; they laughed and spoke vehemently and with great hope of victory.

But on the third day of his father's treatment, Bolbol returned from work to find that the president's portrait had been removed from its usual place on the wall. Abdel Latif gave him no opportunity to ask about it, and Bolbol didn't dare object. He put the picture in his bedroom, but there it kept him up at night. This was odd; it was just a picture, after all, but spending night after night in the same room with it caused Bolbol's worst and most terrifying preoccupations to resume. He covered up the portrait and propped it in a corner of the living room, behind the metal cupboard where he kept his plates. He didn't dare to throw it out or tear it up; he would need it as long as he lived in this neighborhood. Between Bolbol's unwillingness to challenge his father directly, and Abdel Latif's studied avoidance of the topic, they both eventually forgot about it entirely.

Bolbol insisted on closing all the windows in the house for fear that the laughter of his father and the doctor would leak out and catch the attention of someone passing along the alley, who might then stick around to hear their conversations or the revolutionary songs they sang together between bouts of exchanging news from the battlefronts and commentary on political developments. The two of them were agreed that it was a revolution against the entire world, not just against the regime. Abdel Latif still loved big words, and he used plenty of them when describing the things that had happened during the brutal siege, when those who had remained behind had been forced to cook the leaves off the trees and to eat grass. They made bread from chaff, and shared what little they had left.

Their conversations about their inevitable victory conveyed nothing to Bolbol. His only thought was of his father's illness— particularly, how he might rescue himself from the predicament it had caused. Bolbol offered to help his father bathe but was refused; Abdel Latif didn't like seeing himself as a weak old man. Blood analyses showed that his illness was worsening and that hope of recovery was slight. Behind the siege lines, there had been whole months when he hadn't taken his medicine, whole days together that he hadn't eaten. He kept telling Bolbol about the siege, as if asking him not to forget, but Bolbol wanted very much to forget everything that had happened over the past four years. He felt like someone else—a stranger. His father deserved a true son of the revolution, someone brave like Dr. Nizar. The doctor wasn't afraid of being associated with the revolution and had refused to flee the country even after he was arrested and tortured for three months. Bolbol couldn't bear to hear him telling the details to Abdel Latif, who in turn regaled Nizar with tales of the torture undergone by the many other detainees he had known. These prisoners had returned hating the regime more than ever; when they spoke of what they'd endured, it was as though they were implying that revenge was the very least they could do in response. Bolbol's father described in exhaustive terms how, in prison, many had transformed from peaceful revolutionaries to advocates of the utmost violence against the regime and its troops. He added, "Prison can kill you. The person who leaves is not necessarily you, even though they have your appearance." Few retained their self-control and their reason; few remained loyal to their initial ideals. The terrible pressure of each successive story told in Bolbol's house made him wish he were deaf—but he despised himself when he tried to avoid listening. It was only in the final weeks that he really began to worry that his father would die. The day they went to the hospital was the first time that Bolbol really thought about the chaos that could surround a body after death, given the state of things. It didn't even occur to him that his father had been serious about that last wish he had repeatedly extracted Bolbol's solemn promise to carry out.

Bolbol, Hussein, and Fatima successfully made it past the third checkpoint after the town of Deir Atiya, but the bleak road ahead didn't exactly inspire them with confidence. Night was falling, and they had only gotten a quarter of the way: they were nowhere near Anabiya. The same mysterious number from which Bolbol had received his instructions as to where to collect his father on the outskirts of S had called his phone a number of times since that awful day—and now Bolbol was regretting that he'd never picked it up again. He was sure his father's friends wouldn't have let the *ustadh* be buried so far away from them. Perhaps they were even more resourceful than he'd ever guessed, these children of the revolution—they had managed to infiltrate everywhere, communicating by way of a system of secret codes. Maybe those men could have collected the body from anywhere at all and brought it anywhere with no problem. Maybe *they* should have been tasked with arranging the burial. Bolbol was suddenly confident that Abdel Latif's friends could easily have spirited his father's body away from the hospital and buried him in the new cemetery he had himself laid out during the siege in S. Then the dead man would have breathed freely, so to speak.

What did his father's body mean? It was a harsh but justified question that night. All three of them were wondering it, but none had a clear answer. Silence had settled over the minibus. Hussein stayed silent to stifle his anger; Fatima was trying not to breathe, so they would forget she was there. The sounds of missiles and anti-tank bombs were getting closer; Hussein said dispassionately, "They're bombing Homs," before retreating back into his silence. They were all hoping for a miracle to come and save them from this desolation, the fear they couldn't put into words, which burrowed into them all the same. These lulls offered a rare opportunity to talk but always came at inappropriate times, when no one was capable of speaking.

Fatima opened her window again. A cold breeze crept in. She suggested uncovering the body, but neither of her brothers replied, and she wasn't about to reach out herself and draw back the blankets. Instead she tried to mop up some of the water streaming over the floor of the van from the melting ice blocks packed around the corpse. She was frightened, thinking about the terrifying smell oozing from the body's pores, and her fingers were trembling by the time Hussein said they had no choice but to spend the night in the town of Z—but they didn't know which side road to take, and the main highway between Homs and Aleppo had been closed for more than two years.

Hussein turned the minibus in what he thought was the right direction and sped on through the gloom. The road was full of holes, and Bolbol and Fatima held on grimly as the vehicle lurched and almost toppled over. Unable to hold on to anything, the body shuddered. Hussein's rage was evident by now; he tried to call some friends to fix up a place to stay, raised his voice more than once, and eventually halted at the roadside, cursing the unreliable cell signal. Bolbol told him coolly not to worry about where they would stay; they would go to Lamia's house. Fatima's eyes glistened, and she looked at Bolbol sympathetically. Hussein said nothing, but a few minutes later he asked what sort of welcome they were likely to get from Lamia, in her husband's house, after all these years. Bolbol was positive that it would work out, and in fact he only needed to tell Lamia in a steady voice that they would be in Z in a quarter of an hour, and that they needed her help, in order to be proved right. She was as kind and generous as ever, Bolbol thought as he hung up; she had begged them to be careful and promised to wait for them at the entrance to the town with her husband. The checkpoint there had a bad reputation as far as dealing with strangers; they had started filtering out and disappearing travelers who had been forced to pass through the town, or ransoming off the children from rich families.

Bolbol felt oddly powerful; Lamia's voice had energized him. Hussein, meanwhile, felt defeated; he hadn't expected he would need Lamia today of all days. Bolbol had resumed his friendship with her some years earlier. He had met her husband and made a concerted effort to behave like a friend to them both, not an old lover purposely stirring up a husband's jealousy, as Zuhayr, Lamia's husband, had believed at first.

In that first meeting, several years after their graduation, he had invited Lamia and Zuhayr to dinner along with two other couples to celebrate meeting again after so long. Hiyam, Bolbol's wife, and Zuhayr were outsiders in that clique, listening as the ex-classmates laughed and recounted stories of their friends at college. In telling these stories, they realized that, if they were really honest with themselves, not a single one of them had made much of a mark during their student days; they hadn't made trouble, they hadn't protested the administration, hadn't distributed pamphlets for far-right or far-left parties, hadn't tried hashish or lived on the edge in any way. They'd all been rather pathetically well behaved. To conceal this, they conjured up some additional stories about their own small acts of valor—and all conspired to hide the fact that they were merely plagiarizing untold stories from their classmates' biographies.

Bolbol wasn't a source of concern to Lamia's husband, which was all he really cared to know about him at this moment. The men never became close, but neither were they enemies. Bolbol would never have believed that Zuhayr, a powerful man and a former political prisoner, could ever fear a man like himself, who was afraid of his own shadow. Bolbol wished he could close his eyes and relive all his memories with Lamia and, this time, change things. The poems he had written her, the letters with which he had pursued her over summer holidays . . . He'd poured his heart and soul into those poems; he liked to believe that, at the very least, she'd found them too amusing to throw away. If she had stayed with him, he would be a different person entirely, he was sure. Lamia would be sad to hear of Abdel Latif's death; she'd liked him very much. In fact, they had remained close over the years; Lamia would visit or call every now and again, sometimes bringing books by and accepting gifts in return. Equally, she had remained friends with Bolbol's mother, who'd maintained her tradition of cooking *molokhiya* for Lamia—the girl's favorite dish—and she would always insist on giving Lamia a selection of the pickles she was famous for, known locally as Um Nabil's Miracle. Lamia had always found time to visit Bolbol's family, and although these visits grew rarer after graduation, they were a sufficient expression of mutual respect and affection.

Now, crammed into his seat and reviewing all these memories, Bolbol realized that his own pickling skills must have come from his mother. Everything he did was a copy. It wasn't too pleasant to discover that he was just an imitation of his family, repeating throughout his life the very acts he used to despise.

Bolbol said to himself that Lamia was an angel, that she would defend his father's body with all her strength. The soldiers at the checkpoint into Z were irritated at being unable to "interrogate" these strangers as much as they would have liked—the family would have been rich pickings for any checkpoint. Unfortunately for the soldiers, Lamia had informed Zuhayr of the problem posed by the family's identity cards, and he had instantly comprehended the delicacy of the situation. He'd beaten them to the checkpoint, bringing along his uncle, who was connected to influential men in the regime, in order to mediate their swift passage through. Bolbol quickly explained their problems, giving a digest of their adventures to date: the congestion at the checkpoints and their difficulty in leaving Damascus in the first place, adding that they had been traveling now for ten hours. The staff at the checkpoint, a mixture of Mukhabarat agents and volunteers from the town, was unsympathetic but didn't spend too long scrutinizing their papers. They made do with examining the death certificate and then allowed the travelers to pass without even a mutter, though, under other circumstances, and at the very least, the family deserved a good round of cursing out, seeing as they embodied all the necessary qualifications for such—in the view of any checkpoint manned by the Mukhabarat or any of the sectarian groups funded, unofficially, by the regime.

Driving along in the dark, the siblings hadn't noticed the changes that had overtaken the body. Lamia was upset when she saw the current state of it. Everyone was taken aback by her racking sobs, and her tears caused them to weaken as well. Hussein wept, and Fatima saw her opportunity and plunged into a protracted fit of bawling. Zuhayr acted quickly and drove them to the small public hospital. Thanks to his uncle's intercession, the hospital director allowed the body to spend the night in the morgue. The terrible burden was lifted. No one looked at Abdel Latif, afraid of finding his body so disfigured that they would agree to dump it in any hole in the ground—even throw it to the stray dogs.

Lamia was slender as a rail, and her long, thick hair was the color of carob. Her face was innocent, and her smile deeply reassuring. She knew no evil and had been born to give without any expectation of return. Now, after all these years, Bolbol supposed that she regarded him as little more than a sick man in need of her care. When they were younger, however, and parted by distance, she'd read his letters and believed that someone else must have written those texts so full of double entendres and poetic flights of fancy. These letters were the venue in which he could say how much he worshipped her. He wrote that it wasn't right for the throne of a goddess like her to be touched by an ephemeral human—better for eagles to spirit it away while it lay vacant. He still remembered some of his letters by heart, since he'd read and revised and hesitated over them so many times before sending. And then there were the letters he *hadn't* sent, which Lamia didn't even know about—the ones that openly expressed his fervent desire and hunger for her body.

Once, Lamia admitted to him how impatiently she'd waited for his letters throughout the scorching summer holidays in Z, how she was overjoyed when the postman knocked on her family's door and waved a letter at her with a smile. Bolbol had broken into a sweat when she said this and couldn't admit that he loved her to tears. Now he believed Lamia was the only ideal that could salvage his life and perhaps even turn him into a less fragile person.

But he had been too afraid of seeing her hurt to admit all this: the scene of what he assumed would be their inevitable separation haunted his thoughts. He didn't know why, but he was positive it would end badly, that she would say, *I love you, but I can't marry a Muslim.* He hadn't listened to the advice of their mutual friends when they encouraged him to confess his love. They had said that love was more important than marriage; everything else would come later—but on the evening of their arrival at her home, led by her husband, Bolbol felt that he had acted correctly. She wasn't a hard-line Christian, but in the end she would never have wanted to anger her kindhearted, simple country family, who wouldn't have been able to pay for a wedding anyhow. Bolbol quickly warmed up to this reasoning and declared himself well satisfied by his paralysis over the years.

Zuhayr was behaving with his usual gallantry. When Lamia opened the door to her house, Bolbol was struck by how exhausted she looked; he regretted having increased her troubles. More than thirty children were inside, eating dinner. Men and women were coming and going through the four open rooms on the spacious ground floor. That Lamia was hosting displaced people needed no explanation. No one could be surprised by the appearance of strangers; everyone was used to new arrivals crossing their path at any time of day or night. Zuhayr saved the siblings their explanations and simply introduced them as old friends from S on their way to bury their father's body in Anabiya, praising the father as a great revolutionary in the process. Dropping these names was enough of an explanation.

Bolbol was deeply moved by Lamia's sympathetic glances as she held back her tears and accompanied Fatima to the women's room. All three of the siblings looked appalling, but no one noticed or found it unusual; they had all gone through similar ordeals. When she came back, Lamia squeezed Bolbol's hand, pleased that he was carrying out his father's last wish; she described his father as a great man, a martyr, and a revolutionary. She gave Bolbol no time to explain everything they had gone through on the road and went on to say that she was cooking for six families and thirty children, assisting them and making them as comfortable as she could. Zuhayr was kind to the siblings and thanked them for asking if they could help. Really, both husband and wife were like people from another age, Bolbol thought as he watched Zuhayr and Lamia gladly and indefatigably attend to the needs of each of their guests. They were nothing like his neighbors, who had driven out three families, displaced from Yarmouk Camp, on the pretext that they were extremists, probably terrorists, merely because the women wore the hijab. The sight of the expelled made one's heart bleed; but, then, the sight of the impoverished local women was simply sickening. They encouraged their children to pelt the homeless families with stones, yelling curses at these traitors who'd turned their backs on a regime that had housed them, raised them, and educated them in its schools.

Hussein put an abrupt end to the discussion. He asked Lamia for two blankets and a pillow, and after dinner he slipped out to the bus, spread out on its floor, and fell into a deep sleep. Zuhayr suggested to Bolbol, who was grappling with his usual shyness, that he might like to bathe, but added cheerfully that he would have to heat the water in the cistern using firewood, not gas; the electricity only came on for two or three hours a day. Bolbol thanked him and asked for somewhere to lie down. He was so exhausted he could no longer grasp what the men here were saying, passing the time by discussing the latest news or trying to phone someone who had stayed in the besieged city of Homs. The story of their father's body got no sympathy from them; they had seen too many bodies already. As ever, death was so close to them that they had stopped giving it any particular consideration.

Zuhayr generously offered to let Bolbol sleep on his and Lamia's own bed in the corner of the kitchen, but Bolbol chose instead to use a twice-folded blanket for a mattress, then another to cover himself up. He couldn't get over the fact that Zuhayr and Lamia were sleeping here now after giving everything they had to refugees from Homs—total strangers. Lamia repeated Abdel Latif's favorite saying in a low voice: "The children of the revolution are everywhere." Bolbol shut the kitchen door and tried to sleep. He was cold and slow to feel any warmth seep into his body. He tried to push away evil thoughts: Lamia slept here, right there on that bed in the corner of the large kitchen, leaving her bedroom to the children. Here, her breath circulated every night . . . The mattress, only a few centimeters away, smelled strongly of Lamia. Bolbol was bewildered by his growing state of arousal. There was, of course, one way for him to relax—he didn't even feel especially ashamed at the prospect of betraying a man and a woman who had shown him every generosity. After all, the horrific tension was almost killing him, he had no way of sleeping, his senses were inflamed. Even crying would be better than doing nothing; he wished he could manage it. Crying would relax him, wash him clean. And no one would ask a man transporting his father's corpse across the country why he was crying. Bolbol buried his head in his blanket and heard a knocking sound in his head. He began to feel that he would surely die here; in fact, he craved it; Lamia would then bury him with her own beautiful hands—such a terrible tragedy for her! It got to be eleven o'clock at night, and intermingling voices were still coming from the large room where everyone else was gathered as if for a party. He even heard distant laughter. Yes, there was only one way of relaxing. So Bolbol closed his eyes and tried to recall a particular image of Lamia. When they were students, she had brought over some extra course materials for him, and his mother had persuaded her not to head home for Deir Rahibat but to stay the night with them. Bolbol had spied on her at dawn as she was sleeping in Fatima's room. She was like an angel in that bed, her legs revealed by a short cotton nightshirt. Her breasts were firm, and there was the ghost of a smile on her face . . . But now the shame came flooding in. Bolbol scrambled to his feet. He left the kitchen, lit a cigarette, and began to feel calmer. He quieted his conscience; he would sleep, he wanted to sleep, he needed to sleep so he could take his father's body to Anabiya. From there he would cross the border to Turkey and never come back to this country again. What an excellent new idea. He went back to the kitchen and lay down. The voices in the next room receded, and he fell asleep.

Only a couple of hours later, he was shaken awake into a state of instant terror. Hussein was standing by his head, shouting that the nurses were throwing their father's body out into the street. Lamia was waiting for them in the minibus, worried and angry. They had called her to come and take the body away because, once again, the bodies of soldiers killed in a nearby battle were being brought to the hospital.

Zuhayr had gone ahead; as they arrived, they could hear him fighting with one of the nurses who had now taken up cursing their father. Bolbol went into the morgue to sign for the body so Hussein and Zuhayr could carry it back to the bus. It was a terrifying scene. There were more than forty corpses there in military dress; some had lost their lower extremities, others half their heads. A furious officer was speaking to someone out of sight, requesting more ambulances from the hospital in Homs. Bolbol felt sick. He managed to reach the office amid the chaos, but the nurse there didn't understand what he wanted. Bolbol asked for the doctor on duty. The nurses were opening the morgue fridge and piling bodies on top of one another like lemon crates; their tiny fridge hadn't been designed to deal with so many bodies. Bolbol dug through the mound of papers on the office desk and found the release forms.

Clutching these, he looked through the large register, signed his own name next to his father's, and left like he was fleeing hell, almost deranged by fear. If someone thought to ask him for his identity card in all this chaos, he could wind up dead.

On the ground floor of the hospital, a large number of people from the surrounding towns and villages were looking for the bodies of their sons who had died that night. The furious nurse was still cursing Abdel Latif, calling him a terrorist, threatening Zuhayr and Lamia and insulting their whole family. Everyone piled into the minibus, which was thankfully ready to leave. Lamia looked sadly at Abdel Latif's face. It had begun to swell; its skin was turning blue and a shade of green that looked almost moldy. Back at the house they drank coffee while Lamia rewrapped Abdel Latif's shroud, removing the smelly blankets that were still soaked from the slabs of ice and replacing them with clean ones. She also placed sweet basil around the corpse's head, perfumed him all over, and gave Fatima the large bottle of cologne to sprinkle on him from time to time. Then the five of them sat in silence, sipping their coffee, surrounding the dead man, and waiting for dawn.

A BOUQUET FLOATING
DOWN A RIVER

At dawn, the minibus hurried away from Z.

The air was cold, and the cologne wafting through the car put the siblings in a serene state of mind. The feeling that they had the whole day ahead of them made them feel confident of arriving at Anabiya before nightfall. The road was narrow, and the big passenger buses passing alongside them made them less desolate and afraid; they weren't alone out here. The bus passengers looked pitiful, and they seemed to have been traveling a long time. Their clothes were tattered and poor, and desperation had settled on their faces as they stared at the road ahead. Most of the buses were old, their glass windows shattered, and on the backs of each were bundled the possessions of these people fleeing the country for somewhere safer. It was a mass exodus, hundreds of thousands of people heading from the north and the east toward the unknown.

Bolbol closed his eyes and relaxed. The cool breeze had revived him and woke again his longing for the old days with Lamia. He'd felt proud when she had looked at him with affection for carrying out his father's last wish. He had declared to Lamia that he would see to it that Abdel Latif was buried with Aunt Layla (whose story Lamia knew a little about) no matter how dangerous the journey became—saying that he would carry out his father's last wish even if it cost him his life. In front of Lamia, he affected to be careless about his life, as he imagined a brave man might. She wasn't surprised; he had a history of doing idiotic things no one would have believed him capable of.

When Zuhayr had disappeared into prison, who knew where, Bolbol had gone to meet an influential officer, a relative of one of his friends, and asked outright about his whereabouts. Even now Bolbol couldn't forget the quizzical look on the man's face as he sought to clarify the nature of the relationship between Bolbol and Zuhayr. That simple question, asked for the sake of a person he didn't really know, could have consigned Bolbol to an endless nightmare. And Lamia still remembered the night her mother died; she had been astonished to see Bolbol arriving before dawn, wanting to help with the burial. He had traveled all night despite the challenge of finding transport at that time. He had done many things for her over the years, and after the looks of gratitude she had given him he began to feel that he was carrying out his father's instructions solely on her account.

Lamia was one of the few people—perhaps the only one—who gave Bolbol the courage to act recklessly. She never knew it, but his greatest follies had been committed on account of just a few words she'd once spoken in defense of his character, calling him "bold" and "impetuous" when his other friends preferred "indecisive" and "cowardly." Her belief in the courage he in fact lacked had helped him commit more than a few sins in his time (sadly, they went unremembered by all), but despite everything, he had never been brave enough to declare his love for her. Even now his knees started to shake as he imagined what she would say to him: *The right moment for this passed a long time ago.*

Discovering love is like seeing a bouquet floating down a river. You have to catch it at the right time, or the river will sweep it away: it won't wait for long. You have only a few intense, mad moments to give voice to your profound desires. In fact, there had been plenty of bouquets floating tranquilly by, rocking gently close at hand, easily within Bolbol's reach . . . Lamia had waited for him to say something, especially after the long summer holidays were over, but Bolbol stayed silent as usual or merely suggested a walk in Bab Tuma. Eventually she realized that the years she had spent waiting for him to pick up those bouquets floating down the river were over, but despite knowing that they had missed their chance, she didn't conceal her happiness at receiving his letters nor her longing for the next. And so, the thread of their usual conversations would resume where it had been broken by their separation while the river swept the bouquet away.

Whenever she went home for the holidays, she was astonished at the letters that were already waiting for her in her hometown. Bolbol wrote that the very sound of her footsteps was his joy. He even described her handbag in terms borrowed extensively from an ode of the great poet Riyadh al-Saleh al-Hussein. He told her that he had read the poem in question the previous day, on account of her, and on account of her he had also gone to the empty college canteen and sat on their seat in the garden. She replied to every one of his holiday letters, told him how much she missed him, and she didn't bother to hide her happiness at everything he wrote. Sometimes she put a few small wildflowers in her replies, letters that he read dozens of times and kept in a secret place in his closet, afraid they would fall into someone else's hands. For him, these weren't letters but an enormous and personal secret. They were like precious icons hidden in the deepest vaults of a monastery, forbidden and untouched for hundreds of years. As time passed, the secret cast a hidden magic over things; what Bolbol wanted was for Lamia's letters to become enshrined just as he imagined them, a real collection of icons he might suddenly reveal to his future children, after many years, so they would be forced to see their father in an entirely new light.

Yes, he'd missed his chance to pick up that bouquet hundreds of times. Deep down, he still believed that she was a goddess who deserved to be worshipped, not approached. One touch from her was enough for him; he couldn't imagine her as a wife chopping onions, her clothes reeking of cooking smells. But now everything had been lost, regardless, and he was content with what remained of their relationship. Here and now she looked like an angel to Bolbol, an angel reaching out her hand to save the drowning; humanity's only hope lay in her delicate fingers, which could grant life with one affectionate touch.

Bolbol had convinced himself that merely retaining her friendship was a miracle for which he should thank God. He would wait for her to visit Damascus and then take her to the restaurants she loved. Sometimes, and quite intentionally, he took her to places of special importance to their past relationship, where he was tempted to reach out and take her hand. She was polite and friendly to him in those moments, but the silence which soon settled over them made it clear that the past was the past. Then they would return to their favorite topic of conversation when things became awkward: Bolbol would speak and she would listen as he complained about his wife, who thought that buying a new sofa would be preferable to climbing up to the roof of the world and taking in the view. He told her about his wife's repugnant smell, her hardness and utter lack of concern about him. He complained about their sex life; she called the deed "homework" and laughed endlessly at this little witticism. He described her yellow teeth and her never-ending list of demands: fix the boiler, stock up enough fuel for winter, invite her sister and her husband for dinner. Bolbol would then go on to describe what happened whenever the four of them met: his brother-in-law talked constantly about house prices and would end the evening by advising Bolbol in his hoarse voice to convince his father to sell the large family house or to knock it down and build an apartment block so Abdel Latif could sell off the individual apartments. Bolbol didn't know how to extricate himself from this situation, he said, but he never allowed his impatience with his wife or her family to show. He remained the same kind man as ever, who allowed his foolish brother-in-law to appear smart and continually advise him how to arrange his life. Still, Bolbol always concluded this litany by restating his regret at having married a woman who didn't know the poetry of Riyadh al-Saleh al-Hussein—whose conversation consisted entirely of repeating the silly jokes she had been told by colleagues during her trivial day.

As he looked at his shrouded father, Bolbol told himself that he had no regrets at not trying to convince him to sell the house with the flowers Lamia had loved. She used to exchange seedlings with Abdel Latif and spent hours helping him arrange the flower beds. It gave them both indescribable joy, a joy shared by Bolbol's mother, who adored her plants to the point of madness. Bolbol had often observed his mother and father in the garden, lingering over the harvest of their three olive trees. They behaved like the seasonal workers, eating breakfast under the tree and discussing how much of the harvest to give their friends. Bolbol told Lamia that the flowers were a love token between his parents; he meant that they were a secret token of his own love for her, one of many. He didn't dare tell her that he lingered to breathe in the fragrance of every flower she herself had pruned or caressed.

Lamia didn't take too many of the things Bolbol said seriously, but even so, she was an eager listener. He was a different man when he spoke to her; his eyes were bright, his face alive—though he was careful not to be overheard. She knew that he was polite to his brother-in-law, that he didn't argue with his wife but gave in to all her demands. He didn't really care if his wife loved the poetry of Riyadh al-Saleh al-Hussein or not.

Back when Zuhayr was still in prison, Lamia would visit Damascus and insist on spending a lot of time with Bolbol, listening to his complaints. It wasn't that she was getting revenge on him by wallowing in his unhappiness; on the contrary, she sympathized deeply with her old friend. Hearing him, she thought of and enjoyed Bolbol's image of her as an angel. As for herself, she didn't complain: she was strong and didn't want Zuhayr to compromise in exchange for his freedom. She summarized the difficulties caused for her by the Mukhabarat in a few sentences—how they were harassing her at work and in her social circle, which was not really so different from the world of Bolbol's wife. Lamia didn't tell Bolbol that she, too, repeated the same jokes told by all low-ranking public employees, that her house clothes stank of onions, and that she often helped her friends with their simple household errands; equally, she didn't tell him it had been some time now since she last read the poetry of Riyadh al-Saleh al-Hussein, and she never took his diwan down from her bookshelf anymore.

But back when they had graduated and Lamia returned to her hometown and married Zuhayr, her visits grew more and more infrequent, and she lost all interest in those flower beds, just as Bolbol's father lost interest in them after his wife's death. One after another, the flowers withered and died, but Bolbol still tried to enjoy the scent of the rosebushes that Lamia had once tended.

Bolbol used to see his father looking miserably at the garden that had changed so utterly, staring with grief in his heart. For him, it had become a place that spoke only of loss, a leftover from a happier and vanished age. After his wife's death, Abdel Latif changed considerably; he no longer cared much about little details, and the things in his life all lost their shine. He refused Fatima's offer to clear the closet of her mother's clothes and many belongings, and he became suspicious that she might do it in his absence. His misgivings increased dramatically whenever Fatima visited him; he would lock the door to her mother's room and put the key in his pocket. He wouldn't even allow anyone to clean it unless he was present, a clear sign that he wanted his memories left undisturbed, or so it seemed to everyone. He spent a lot of time reading history and sitting silently in front of the television. He wished he would die, but death wouldn't grant his wish, no matter how much he pleaded. He spent five years in this way, longing for death as if he and his wife had made a secret pact to depart this life together, although when at last she had deserted him, he had simply let her go.

After his wife's death, Abdel Latif rarely referred to the dear love he had just buried. He didn't mention her much or reminisce about the details of his life with her, as if he had lost the vocabulary to speak of his happier past. No one doubted seventy-year-old Abdel Latif's love for his wife. Everything was proof of it: the rarity of their fights, the way they clung to each other—the image of the happy family (so much like all other happy families) that they projected wherever they went. But Bolbol often thought that the true meaning of love was what he had never experienced and what was now lost to him. He was reminded of all this when he first brought his ailing father back to his house. Bolbol examined him closely; he would almost have sworn that this man wasn't his father. Starvation had left its scars on his aged body, and his eyes had an odd gleam to them. Abdel Latif wasted no time in telling Bolbol that he had distributed his mother's clothes to the few neighbors who had stayed behind during the siege. And, by the way, the garden had returned to its former splendor, though now all it grew was basil and wormwood, not counting the three olive trees, which he hoped would hold out for a few more years at least. He added, "Nevine and the martyrs love wormwood." Without giving Bolbol time to ask, his father told him neutrally that he had married her, Nevine, and that she was the one who had pushed him to escape the besieged town. She had told him resolutely, "Leave this sacred ground." His father was silent for a long time before carefully addressing Bolbol's questions over the next few days. Bolbol was very frightened and didn't fully grasp what his father had said that night.

The next day Bolbol had wondered about the connections between Nevine, the martyrs, and the wormwood. He told the doctor who'd accompanied him that his father was a little delirious, but the doctor discovered that his patient, although on his deathbed, was fully alert and not delirious in the least.

Of course, Bolbol understood why his father had distributed his mother's clothing; after all, what would a man on the brink of death do with the clothes of a woman who had died several years earlier? The people under siege shared everything—food, clothes, whatever they had that would keep them alive. But his father surprised him when he added the following night that every door should be thrown open to love, that love could sweep away the past all at once, which had helped to cleanse his being and strip away the withered branches that would never put out leaves again. It was agonizing, of course, to slice off your awful past and throw it away, but it was necessary if you were to catch the bouquet of roses floating down the river and carry it safely to the other side . . .

Bolbol had thought his father might be raving, because he was speaking in clear but disjointed phrases, like people do when suffering from partial memory loss or maybe while sifting through a surfeit of memories, the whole tumultuous chaos of the last four years. Bolbol listened with a lump in his throat; he considered his mother's clothes to be his father's business, and of his own accord he relinquished his own stake in whatever other household goods could be divided up between Fatima and Hussein. Meanwhile, his memories of Lamia never left him; what remained of them would have to sustain him. He felt empty and couldn't sleep that night, thinking of the unsent letters to Lamia he had kept. Over the following days, he began to empathize with his father for the first time—his suffering had been kept hidden for years.

Forty-five years earlier, Nevine had been a lovely woman. She entered the teacher's lounge one day and without any ado introduced herself as the substitute art teacher. Abdel Latif stared with a passion that embarrassed her. He had been searching for love at first sight and believed he had found it at last. A few days later, Nevine opened up about her background: she was a university student at the Faculty of Fine Arts in Damascus; she was teaching art to cover her course fees. Her father was a math teacher and her mother a primary-school teacher in al-Mayadin. Her family lived in the village of Muhassan near Deir Azzour, known as Little Moscow. Nevine had chosen to live in a small house in the meadows around S. She was nice to her students. Abdel Latif would wait until she was entering or leaving the school to waylay her, inventing some excuse for conversation. He told her about the geography and history of the Euphrates, and Nevine responded politely, merely confirming that his information was correct, in much the same way she replied to the blandishments of all her male colleagues—something about her accent, from the Euphrates region, made them all try to flirt with her. But she wouldn't allow anyone into her private life, which was much quieter than was suspected by her small-town neighbors and the bachelor teachers. Quite simply, she was a middle-class girl from an educated family, conservative in most things, despite her clothes, which spoke of a liberality and particularity that, nonetheless, no one found especially provocative. When she wandered around S, which at that time was a small town of no more than ten thousand people, she seemed the archetypal *fellaha* from some distant village, rather than a painter fighting against tradition.

Abdel Latif didn't dare to be frank about his feelings, much less his ambition to marry her. He lay awake at night, feeling as though he were drowning in a gray and indescribable space, somewhere between love and desire. There in S, everyone was a villager, each about the same as the others, but Nevine was the exception—her every quality struck him as entrancing: her beautiful voice when she sang old Iraqi songs, and her great kindness, made her seem like a leaf in an autumn gale.

The first three months after they met had been the most difficult for Abdel Latif. He was always trying to hint to Nevine how he felt about her: to signal all his pleasure and fear. True, he had trouble believing that this girl who taught three days a week and spent the rest of her time in art school was really as innocent as she looked, but he didn't care. He believed that she liked him back, but was too anxious to find out for sure, and so went on loving her silently and sleeplessly.

He went to Anabiya as usual to spend the fortnight's holiday with his family, who no longer objected to his choice to live so far away from them—indeed, for years now his family had done its best to make him feel welcome and tiptoed around any subject that might annoy or enrage him. The subject of his sister Layla was closed—the family no longer mentioned her at all. Her story might be too painful to be forgotten, but everyone was willing to try. They conspired to efface it by concocting fairy tales to cover the truth, relying on the sound principle that if you really want to erase or distort a story, you should turn it into several different stories with different endings and plenty of incidental details. They said, for example, that Layla had committed suicide because she suffered from incurable leprosy or that she was hideous and had been concealing a congenital defect since birth, and the legend that she had been a beautiful girl was a lie. The most horrible story is always the one that people believe, in the end, but nevertheless, the truth never dies, even if its voice is so faint no one can hear it. The true story was perfectly clear to those with ears to hear it: Layla was beautiful and strong-willed, and she refused to accept the humble, cringing life others had chosen for her. Instead, she had made a choice of her own—to die.

Abdel Latif returned from his holiday firmly convinced that Nevine wasn't some brief infatuation. Her smile had never left him for a single instant. He felt like a man who not only hadn't caught the bouquet floating down the river but had dived into the river's depths and drowned. He resolved to make a clean breast of all this to her after his return to S and was therefore somewhat taken aback to find that his dear friend Najib Abdullah had married Nevine while he was away.

Without preamble, Najib had gone to Muhassan with his whole family in tow and asked Nevine's family for her hand. Everything was settled without difficulty. They were married, and Nevine moved into her husband's house in the middle of his family's large estate. Everything was as it should be, apart from Abdel Latif's suffering, which accumulated in devastating silence. Nevine was the only one who ever caught the least sign of that suffering, especially during the big party the couple threw to celebrate their marriage. Abdel Latif couldn't hide his longing for her, nor his overwhelming regret at being too late to have caught the bouquet. She ignored him then, and it was years before she sought him out to lessen the torments of this man who had loved her for so long.

Everything was concluded without fuss. Despite her unhappiness in her marriage, she never admitted to having made a mistake she, too, would silently regret. She'd known that Abdel Latif wasn't the man for her; she liked him well enough, but not enough to marry and live with him. For several months after her wedding Abdel Latif did nothing, and remained alone, striving to get over his wound. He avoided Nevine and made excuses whenever his friend Najib Abdullah invited him around—Najib, who never even noticed that he'd stolen the girl his friend hoped to marry. But then there was a lot Najib didn't know: he was also unable to see that he was living with a woman who dreamed strange dreams and possessed a sensitivity so exquisite as to be excessive. To Najib, everything was normal; his mother had pointed this woman out, so he broached the topic of marriage with her, and Nevine didn't refuse. Everything was soon over and done with, and life went on smoothly and happily. It wasn't long before monotony imposed the rhythm of forgetfulness on everyone but Abdel Latif. Her perfume, even at a distance, still stirred him, her walk dazzled him, and at times her penetrating eyes threatened to destroy his defenses and expose his weakness. Nevine forgot all about her own art; she became a normal mother and teacher, accepting the duties of her lot without complaint. Within a few years she was like all the other women of S; she never used her beautiful voice, forgot her Iraqi songs, and even lost her sweet accent, which now only slipped out on rare occasions.

Bolbol found it all hard to believe. He just couldn't think of his father as a lonely, unrequited lover. At last he understood the secret of Abdel Latif's love for Iraqi songs! For whenever Nevine abandoned something from her past, Abdel Latif reflexively picked it up and kept it, polishing it anew and storing it in some remote corner of his life. He kept many of Nevine's old paintings, dusting them off and rescuing them from decay where they had been left in the school storeroom. And yet, despite everything, this same supposedly sensitive man berated Bolbol bitterly when the latter slunk back to the family seat after his divorce, the bereaved man showing a cruelty in the midst of his grief that Bolbol found unbearable.

This return to the family home was supposed to lighten the

suffering of both the widowed father and the divorced son. Lamia, when she visited them, couldn't bear to see Abdel Latif so bereft as he marked five years after his wife's death. He wouldn't indulge her suggestion of taking him back to her village for a long visit, even though she declared with enthusiasm that it was more than fitting given the closeness of their friendship, adding that a long visit would delight Zuhayr and their two children, too, and that perhaps Abdel Latif could help her revive her parsley. He just looked at her and smiled, then went off to prepare dinner. He told her, "When your beloved goes away, they take the keys of happiness with them and throw them into that deep pit known as the grave." His wife hadn't left him any happiness, he said, but had taken everything with her: sleep, the secrets of cooking, their morning coffees together and evening walks through the town. Now he was abandoned, alone, waiting to die—she had taken everything with her. Not that he told Lamia about his depression—and he'd never told anyone that it had been forty years since he had last tasted happiness, on that holiday to Anabiya when he was dreaming about Nevine. No, for him, everything was finished. His memories of his wife were a simile, so to speak—an interregnum, no more, resembling love—before he could be with his true beloved. So much time had passed, and Nevine was still surprised by Abdel Latif's occasional furtive glances; most oddly, in recent years these glances had begun to break through her reserve, leaving her bewildered. From her depths, pleasant feelings surfaced that she couldn't describe.

Surrendering to one's memories is the best way of escaping the wounds they preserve; constant repetition robs them of their brilliance and sanctity. So as the minibus was leaving the checkpoint at Z, that's just what Bolbol did, swamped with pain as he was, feeling as though he were sinking into the earth . . . The morning was serene, and a peculiar silence had settled after a night of intense bombardment, but they knew it wouldn't last the closer they got to the zones where the fighting had been at its most intense for two and a half years. The opposition forces had captured the principal roads, weakening the regime forces and threatening their supplies of fuel and wheat . . . Bolbol tuned out and once more revisited his father's last nights in his house. Abdel Latif had been exhausted and overcome with pain; he knew he wouldn't survive, and again a vehement desire to die seized him and never left him.

His father spoke in a faltering voice about death and love, about the revolution and the martyrs, about the great future waiting for the children who had been born in these past four years and those who were yet unborn. An image of his wife returned to him, but he didn't linger on it for long. He prayed for mercy on her soul in a few conventional phrases, just as people did before the war when a stranger's funeral passed by. He elaborated on his relationship with his beloved Nevine. Bolbol understood this desire to narrate everything all over again, to reveal a side of himself that no one had known. Abdel Latif wanted to leave his final story in Bolbol's hands—not only his final wish. Abdel Latif was increasingly cheerful as the day drew nearer when he would lie in Layla's grave. He still missed her, in spite of everything, and was delighted whenever he heard the fantastic stories that star-crossed lovers wove around her, although they personally preferred to live loveless rather than die for their grand romantic dreams. These failed lovers, this host of ordinary men and women who had surrendered to the ways of this cruel earth, considered Layla their patron saint. They left roses on her neglected grave in secret, composed songs to her, and described her savage beauty with endless fascination.

Abdel Latif may have stopped mentioning the mother of his children, but nevertheless Bolbol recalled that his father had been assiduous in visiting her grave on holidays, as custom demanded. Still, the decades they had lived together were enough. Nevine compensated him for all his losses and had restored life to his soul and his body. The dead are more comfortable when they're buried beside their loved ones; they speak to one another in a secret code impenetrable to the living. If it wasn't for his sister Layla, and Nevine's wish that Abdel Latif be far away from her when he died and was buried, he wouldn't have asked to be interred in Anabiya. Nevine had refused to allow him to be buried in the same grave as her. How could he have found rest among the graves of her son and her husband, Najib Abdullah, his old friend? Several times he asked her to reconsider and allow him to stay close to her, as he wanted to die in her arms, but she wouldn't discuss the matter. She wasn't interested in surviving any more loved ones. She had no intention of being a custodian for any more graves.

Nevine had begun to believe that she would be around for many more years to come. This abundance of time dazed her. Nothing would satisfy her save going back to the land of her childhood. She wanted to cast off everything that might hamper her from flying freely away down that lengthy road lined with meadows . . . She liked to think that there she would go back to singing the sad songs of her childhood that befitted her two martyred sons; there she would be rid of her burdens, and everything superfluous would be shed. Men were plentiful everywhere; there was no use getting attached to one. Abdel Latif couldn't change her mind, even as she moved in with him. The most wretched of creatures are those who are worshipped; what Nevine wanted was something far better: to be someone who worshipped and adored, not just another beloved worshipped by someone who adored her. She realized why she had always been miserable: she had never been a lover herself.

And so, Abdel Latif kept insisting that Bolbol be his audience during his last days. Bolbol alone knew about his father's secret love; he imagined Hussein's shocked expression when he discovered that the family home in S was to be split four ways instead of three—the only inheritance remaining to them.

One morning, Abdel Latif woke up early, eyes bright and face flushed. The previous night he had spoken to Nevine over a satellite phone belonging to a squadron commander he knew well. He'd beamed when he saw that there was an unknown number on the line, and he closed the door of his room behind him, emerging cheerfully a few minutes later to say that he would go to sleep early that night, after which he went right back into his room. This shyness struck Bolbol as rather peculiar, under the circumstances. In the morning, he found his father drinking coffee in the kitchen, and Bolbol's cup was already waiting for him. His father surprised him by saying that if he'd lived much longer, he would have been nothing but the caretaker of the martyrs' graveyard, which he had constructed himself. He cared for the plants and the flowers and the trees and listened to the raucous laughter of the departed martyrs every night. He spoke to them about their blood, which hadn't been spilled in vain; he told them how the tyrant would soon depart, and children would go to school in clean clothes again, with heads held high and eyes filled with faith in their future. He spoke to Bolbol about martyrdom and revolution, confident in victory, and he didn't want to hear any criticism. When Bolbol made his opinion clear, saying that the revolution was over and had become a civil war, and how the regime's superior army would win in the end, his father made do with shaking his head and smoking voraciously without comment, ignoring what his son was telling him. Bolbol was irritated at being ignored and wanted to add that the international community—Russia, America, and all the West—was agreed that the regime should stay and that it would outlast this orphaned revolution, but Abdel Latif was done with the conversation, seeing how it would only corrupt his dreams. He didn't want to be cruel to his son, but made it clear that he was here to talk and Bolbol here to listen, nothing more; in a few days he would be far away, and then Bolbol could go back to his opinions and his capitulation, could go on living in a neighborhood supporting the regime. He could dance to the sectarian songs broadcast by the speakers fixed above the houses where Hezbollah agents, who no longer hid their faces, gathered openly with National Defense troops—militias that the regime had recruited and armed, made up of volunteers, mostly regime supporters and Iraqi Shi'ites. Most members of these militias were unemployed or had criminal records, and no restraint was placed on their capacity to insult, arrest, and murder at will. They inspired terror even in fellow loyalists.

When Bolbol passed them, he greeted them as cheerily as he could manage; he tried to smile and never let his voice falter in calling out to them. His father, on the other hand, once spat on the ground in a clear show of defiance and said to Bolbol, "These traitors and invaders should all drop dead." Bolbol tried to hurry their pace. He begged his father to stop his puerile behavior. Militias like these could kill anyone without having to answer for it. He told his father a dozen stories about what they had done to people, especially families who were sympathetic to the revolution. For instance, they burned down a family's house when they discovered the son had been arrested at a checkpoint for smuggling medicine into the areas of Homs still under siege. On another occasion they kidnapped a girl from a neighboring district who died after being raped continuously for four days, and her family was forced to officially declare that she had died in a road accident if they wanted to get her body back. The neighbors stayed silent; deep down, many approved of the punishment her family had received. No one came to mourn with the girl's family after her body was thrown into their living room, wounds still fresh. The family couldn't bear to stay and left for Argentina to join distant relatives of the girl's father. As for the father himself, he refused to leave the country before getting revenge on his daughter's murderers, whom he knew by name. He returned to his hometown near Homs and shut himself away there, waiting for the moment when he could point a gun in the faces of the murderers. He hung a list of their names on his wall.

Bolbol did his best to avoid hearing such stories, but some still managed to reach him. Somehow his ordinary, enormous baseline level of fear had managed to worsen since his father came to stay. He believed that the walls containing his usual fear—like a musty, battle-scarred citadel—had finally been knocked down, and he was falling into open space. He couldn't keep it up forever; living in this neighborhood made him pay for his life twice over. He was deeply lonely, and at the same time didn't want to belong to any community. He was far from neutral in his mind: for example, he couldn't stop himself from feeling cheered whenever he saw a funeral procession for the regime's casualties pass by. He couldn't meet their eyes in the posters hung on city walls declaring them to be martyrs. But fear prevented him from even gossiping with his coworkers when they gloated over the growing worries of the regime's supporters, who were also beginning be afraid. Fear had become the only true opposition; it was now each individual versus their own fear, and no one trusted the regime any longer. The ongoing impasse was too terrible to be endured, and everyone had begun to speak of their fear openly. Anyone who had been confident of victory a year before began to feel powerless and weak, increasingly vulnerable, even in mortal peril. Since he was incapable of close observation of anyone else, Bolbol kept an eye on himself, only to discover that he was the most craven of all.

In the final months of 2013, the city had begun to feel a new pressure that no one could explain. In rare moments of clarity, Bolbol would say to himself that it was due to the idea of revenge, pure and simple, taking alarming root in the regime; it no longer wanted to win so much as to punish. He mused sardonically on this dreadful idea: he would wake up one day and see his street empty, everyone having run for their lives. The district chief had already fled, having spared no effort in surveilling every inhabitant of the neighborhood during his tenure. He wrote reports on all the suspicious characters there, including his own relatives, as had the young men who weren't content with supporting the regime but carried weapons and insulted their childhood friends and generally made everyone's life hell. Suspicions alone were enough to lead to corpses lining the streets. Suspicions alone were enough to cause someone to disappear without a trace.

Bolbol didn't ask many questions, frightened of getting tangled in the same net of hatred and turning into yet another person bent on revenge. He would find a means of getting rid of his fear, he told himself, but it was difficult to get rid of the thought of revenge. It wasn't even enough for your enemy to be dead for the fire of vengeance to be extinguished; you had to be the one to murder him yourself if your bloodlust was ever to be satisfied. It was terrifying to see such sentiments no longer hidden but plainly written on silent faces expressing nothing but wrath.

His father regretted leaving the land of the martyrs, as he proudly called his village. He wanted to sit quietly that night, but he was afraid of dying with Bolbol's defeatist talk being the last words he heard from his weak, used-up son. He got up, went to the kitchen, and began to peel some potatoes; despite being clearly exhausted he was resolved to fry some the way Nevine made them. He cheered himself up by returning once again to her story, caring little that Bolbol found it painful to think of her as his father's second wife and sweetheart, not Auntie Nevine, the wife of his father's old friend. Afterward, Bolbol had the ridiculous idea of avenging his mother somehow . . . and then he fantasized about doing the same thing with Lamia if Zuhayr died: this time he would kneel at her feet and beg to be allowed to remain at her side. He used to think that love meant a happy old age with your beloved—as if the years before that were worth nothing, merely something to be gotten through in order for the lover to reach the moment when his torment would stop, a new life would begin, and the daydreams he had enjoyed hundreds of times in his warm bed would be reconstructed in reality. Happy were those who spent their old age with their lover. Old age was a deliberate reliving of childhood, and the time that separated these stages was just a distraction, however long it lasted, even if this meant years had to be willfully squandered before you could begin to understand their superfluity. This is what happened to his father when he met Nevine again. As for her, she didn't need much time to think over his proposal. Mainly she was surprised by his folly. She'd thought that things between them had died, or else grown so obsolete that they could no longer mean anything to anyone. A few indirect comments weren't a declaration of love under any circumstances—just as some shy and occasional glances were hardly a confession of desire.

She was astonished that Abdel Latif could still describe the first time she entered the school. He remembered the color of her socks, the style of her shoes, her white blouse and black skirt. He was eloquent in describing her perfume, the shape of her neck, her laughter, and the color of her eyes. He only left off describing each detail in order to return to it a moment later, this time more vehemently. Nevine was bewildered. She didn't mask her longing for the days when S was still a small village crossed by one long, straight road, when it was surrounded by groves of olives, peaches, and apricots and grapevines. Its houses were spacious and welcoming then, the doors were always left open, and you could count the number of strangers on one hand. It was only a few kilometers from Damascus, but the road to the city used to be lined with meadows, of which only a few remained now.

She liked to have someone from those times around to reminisce with. In truth, she'd barely paid any attention to those attractions back when they'd really existed, but now she liked to give them central, undisputed pride of place in her memories. She'd had another life in art school that no one from S knew about, but in the end, it hadn't been enough for her. That life consisted of a single failed love story, adolescent in its simplicity. She had been in love with the same young man as all the girls in her university class. She was the first to withdraw from the race, unable to bear being so totally ignored. Withdrawal suited her conservative personality and her lack of self-confidence, frightened as she was of the passions and caprices of the city. She guarded this story closely, considering it a dangerous secret, a failed sexual adventure, a one-time-only experience. Her reticence went unappreciated by her colleagues at the art college, where disorder and stupidity were an integral part of student life.

She thought of the long night when she met Abdel Latif again. They were both caring for a young man who had been hit by a sniper bullet, which had ripped through his shoulder. His prognosis was good, and there was no real cause for concern. The battle had stopped for some days, but the truce wouldn't last. Everyone could see the hordes of regime forces at the entrances to the town; tanks and defense artillery had been stationed there, checkpoints made of sandbags had sprung up, and snipers had proliferated on every tall building that overlooked the town. That night there was a full moon, and everything was quiet. Abdel Latif had spent days rearranging every detail in the field hospital. He made a list of all the medications in the stores as well as the names of the patients who had been discharged, along with the casualties whose burials he organized meticulously in the new graveyard he'd built, with numbered graves. When preparing this new cemetery for the victims of the siege, he made sure to gather flowers for them all—something that caused Nevine to reflect that this man must have changed considerably since she'd last seen him. He seemed different from the other men his age: younger, more vigorous. Nothing frightened him anymore. He would rush into the heat of battle alongside the young men and drag the wounded to safety, heedless of dying himself. A strange energy welled up from inside him, and despite his long workdays he made do with only a few hours of sleep a night and never forgot a single detail required by the field hospital or the graveyard.

She felt him panting like a teenager, and it wasn't long before he reached for her hand and squeezed it with disconcerting force. She thought it was just an expression of the solidarity called for in such circumstances, but even so she felt a not-entirely-innocent sensation flowing through her veins. He would never find a better opportunity than this to declare the love he felt compelled to reveal. He talked for more than an hour, and Nevine listened without comment—not that he gave her any chance to respond, to correct his interpretation of the facts he related with such confidence; he just stood up when he was finished and walked out. He left the hospital for what remained of his house: a single bedroom and the remnants of the kitchen, whose eastern wall had been destroyed, leaving it open to the garden. He was used to living in these ruins and refused to leave the house; he told his friends, who asked him to move somewhere safer—somewhere with a cellar that might protect him from the aerial bombardment—that whatever remained of his own home was good enough for him. He wouldn't leave his bed; to do so would make him feel like a stranger to himself. Homesickness always began with leaving one's bed, he said, and abandoning the little items you use every day that have become a part of you. Leaving these objects behind is extremely difficult and is always a herald of misfortune.

He wasn't the only man who refused to leave his shell of a home, but even so his determination to stay put seemed incomprehensible. His remaining friends and acquaintances explained it as reluctance to leave his memories of his wife, but the truth was that Abdel Latif didn't want to leave the place where, for years, he had daydreamed about Nevine. The night of his confession, he slept deeper than he had for years, while Nevine sat alone on her bench in the garden of the field hospital, unable to move. She thought of what Abdel Latif had said and tried to piece together his precise words, the various expressions he had used. She couldn't remember anything in concrete terms, but she had to admit that the thought of shaking up her life was attractive. She was delighted to discover there were men who had been in love with her for years without speaking a word to her about it; she'd always hated being the country girl afraid of the city who hadn't felt able to turn down the first suitable offer of marriage. And after accepting, she hadn't been able to back out; Najib Abdullah never gave her a logical enough reason for retreating from her foolish decision, agreeing to be joined to a man she didn't love. She hadn't noticed that life had already presented her with a bouquet floating quickly down the nearby river; she hadn't seen it until it was too late, when it didn't mean anything anymore. What was the point of clinging to memories as life went by? They were only good for digging up more pain, she thought.

Abdel Latif didn't pursue her, exactly, but neither could she forget what he'd said. He was always present nearby, like a moth fluttering around her. He had decided to burn; no more slow living for Abdel Latif—that was what he thought as he saw her furtive looks at him changing every day. He felt surrounded by a wall of time protecting him from frustration and sluggishness. He was confident she wouldn't let him drown in the whirlpool again. He didn't know where he found the courage to act so recklessly in the early years of the revolution, doing so many things he used to find horrifying. He opened his wife's wardrobe, and the smell of moldy clothes wafted in his face. Even now he refused to look inside. He asked a girl who took care of donated goods to cart everything away, and he cleared the house of his wife's clothes at last. Later he decided that this wasn't enough; he asked a group of young men to take the whole wardrobe out of the house and dispose of it; some nails in the wall would be enough to hang his few clothes on. *If you want to expel someone from your memory, you need to remove their scent from your presence entirely.*

He asked himself: What do the martyrs need? Nothing, was

his reply, and he went on: Even if they were alive, nothing. He liked the idea of renunciation and asceticism in these times, the same way he liked seeing himself as a living martyr seeking death at every moment, a man who had truly destroyed the walls of fear by reviving a cherished notion: that of the brave man who couldn't have cared less about that cruelest of all humanity's fears—death. He kept a vial of poison in his pocket, small but enough for a quick death, and planned to swallow it if he were ever arrested. He wouldn't give them the pleasure of torturing him. He thought of all the courageous people he had read about in the histories of various other revolutions who had climbed the scaffold without faltering, spitting on their murderers and striding forward into oblivion with total composure and resolution.

Meanwhile, Nevine thought for a long time about all she had left: nothing but graves. Once again, she was an outsider longing for her childhood home. Her sons' friends tried to alleviate her loneliness, but how to carry on living was the greater problem. Basically, there was no one left; at night the town was completely desolate. A few thousand people still clung on, but they couldn't go outside after curfew. Few houses had completely escaped destruction, and the town had become communal property; what remained wouldn't sustain anyone for more than a few weeks. Supplies were exhausted; animals were dead; water pipes and electric wires were completely destroyed. Everyone was thinking up other ways of surviving, with never a moment free from considering the question of how to keep clinging on to life. They had to dig up old wells, remember the old ways of storing the beans that grew wild around the edges of the nearby meadows. Reaching the distant fields full of produce had become impossible; regime troops had closed off all the entrances and exits to the town, and four large military campaigns had allowed them to occupy observation posts and embed large groups of snipers around the place who kept watch over every possible—and impossible—way of reaching the fields.

Everyone wanted to smash their mirrors. It was hard enough looking at other people's faces without feeling miserable, let alone one's own. They had heard about starvation from books and fairy tales, but now they were experiencing it for themselves, along with selfishness and a new lust for survival. People fought fiercely over a handful of herbs and a few wild mushrooms. Everything had changed in the small town, and what had been normality a few months earlier now became unimaginable. Abdel Latif walked the empty streets among the destroyed houses, looking for some scrap of food that might have been forgotten, a few handfuls of bulgur wheat or rice, a little corn or olive oil, the remains of some ground lentils, but he never found anything, as others had been there before him. He spent hours combing through the rubble, walking through nearby scrubland looking for anything edible: rabbit, dog, cat—anything would do, and everything had become acceptable. People slaughtered dogs and invented new recipes for them; they drove cats out of every corner. Many people died of starvation. He didn't want to go home empty-handed; the sweetheart waiting for him there was withering away with each passing day. Their late-woken feelings helped them both to find their innocence once again; they knew all the phases of the moon and kept watch for each.

Because Nevine hadn't kept him waiting long. She said that she didn't want to spend the rest of her life alone. Abdel Latif understood her well enough.

That day was in the winter of 2013, two weeks before Christmas. Abdel Latif had been to the church earlier in the afternoon—

it had been substantially destroyed in the last bombardment. Father Walim had been one of the last Christians to leave before the siege finally closed around the town, and he had charged Abdel Latif with looking after what remained of the church, reassuring him that the archbishop had already moved all the manuscripts and icons to an unknown location in Lebanon. Abdel Latif understood him well enough, too: he had to care for the soul of the place—that was his task. So every now and then he would go there and wander around the rubble. Only a small part of the large hall was still standing, and in the middle of it a door led to a narrow room holding priests' robes and some small bottles of oil. Abdel Latif was astonished that these had been left untouched; the looters hadn't spared anything else—not even the huge bell this church and all the other churches in the area used to boast of. Syrian ironmongers had made it especially for a church in Antakya, but they were so proud of their craftsmanship they didn't want to see it hanging so far away, and so they hid it instead. A few years later they gifted it to the church in S, where they could enjoy its peals every Sunday.

Abdel Latif went inside and spent some time reading a book he found in the rubble; the book was torn, but there was still a possibility its binding could be repaired. When he left the church in the evening, Nevine was sitting on a large boulder outside, waiting for him. He was surprised to see her there. He sat beside her, and she repeated that she didn't want to spend the rest of her life alone. The two of them went quiet and didn't move. Then Abdel Latif took hold of her hand and kissed her timidly. He pulled her into an embrace, and they sank into a long kiss; Abdel Latif immediately considered it the only real kiss in his life. Still, they both acted quite properly. They stood up and went to the house of their friend

Sheikh Abdel Sattar and asked him to marry them. Nevine invited the few remaining friends of her sons to witness the signing of the marriage contract.

Happily, a few people were still around to celebrate the wedding with them—the front lines were relatively quiet that night, so there was no need for every man to be at his post. The wedding was perfectly ordinary, and not in the least bit strange, as Nevine had feared—it was simply an occasion for joy. Fighters fired into the air to celebrate the newlyweds, and no one who remained in the town—sharing their hunger, thirst, and cold, caring for the graves of the martyrs—refused Ustadh Abdel Latif's invitation. He felt a powerful sense of renewed connection to everything, and there were new, different feelings now, too, driving away the image of himself he'd been nursing all these years—an elderly man killing time as he waited to die. He took up once more all his old and powerful ideals about revolution and living an honorable life. Deep down he felt himself to be fortunate; he would witness the end of a regime that had brought him nothing but shame since his youth. His former party comrades had betrayed every principle and pounced upon every advantage, had imprisoned their old friends for years at a time, and hadn't hesitated to sell out their cause to stay in power.

Life settled down after the siege closed around the town. Abdel Latif no longer had anything to do but pass the time. He planted flowers on graves and in the walkways of his graveyard, which he hadn't expected to grow so huge. He organized everything, numbering the graves and recording every detail in a large register: the names of the victims, how they had died, their last words, their family names and ID numbers, and a full description, including height, eye color, skin tone, and any distinguishing marks. Perhaps no one would stay in town for much longer, he used to think, but the day would come when they would all return, and when they did, they should know where their loved ones were buried. He didn't know why people would want to know this, as such, but considered running the graveyard a sacred duty just the same; the living looked after themselves well enough.

Despite starvation, everyone still clung to hope and spoke optimistically about the days to come. They realized that despair meant drowning in the abyss, so kept faith with the confidence that was the only possession they had left. The regime, with all its might behind it, inflicted unimaginable losses in every battle, but the people of S couldn't retreat; they had burned all their bridges.

Nevine was surprised she was still capable of doing so much. She would talk animatedly about her previous life, and Abdel Latif would listen sympathetically. He lit candles for her every night, and they would reorder the place afresh. Outside they would move lightly among the ruins, exchanging kisses in the abandoned, shattered houses. They took shelter from a rain shower under a roof, embracing each other as though they might be separated at any moment. They had no time to search for the right term to define their new life together even though they both liked big words. They relished all the small details they had been missing in their lives. They went hungry with each other and with everyone else, and they gathered grasses and concocted soups out of narcissus bulbs and nameless herbs. They hoarded salt carefully, made bread from whatever remnants of lentils, chickpeas, or beans were available, or really out of anything that could make up for the flour that was usually missing. The usable roads linking S to a nearby town that wasn't under siege were secret and few, and they brought in only a small quantity of medicine and flour. Abdel Latif and Nevine didn't approve of the monopoly that the fighting men had on the majority of the smuggled goods, but they didn't have time to find fault or to fight over a handful of flour. They worked vigorously to plant Abdel Latif's garden with vegetables they could dry and store, such as beans, eggplants, tomatoes, and a few ears of corn; under siege, one didn't have the luxury of choice.

Nevine couldn't shake off her fear of winding up alone. Abdel Latif no longer gave her the time or space to talk freely about her past life; they had discussed the past enough to forget it. He was always keeping her occupied with daily plans, and she soon fell in with him and entered enthusiastically into their new life. She joined him in making butterfly nets and ran behind them like a small child, indifferent to the bombs and missiles exploding incessantly nearby. She was convinced that the best way of beating the war was to stop talking about it. She had stopped being afraid of dying a long time before and was even more reckless than Abdel Latif, who would rush off to the front lines swinging a first-aid kit at the least provocation. Nevine would walk calmly through the empty streets, looking at the bombs raining down over the town, and the only thought she gave them was this: They won't kill anyone, unless it's from fear. There was no one left for the bombs to blow up, after all. They'd already murdered everyone there was to murder; now they were destroying only already destroyed houses. The fighters could protect themselves well enough by digging long trenches and erecting secret fortifications, shoring up their already strong defense lines. In the end, though, war is war, and it wouldn't be over easily or quickly. It carried its stench with it wherever it reached, wafting over everyone, leaving nothing as it had been. It altered souls, thoughts, dreams; it tested everyone's capacity for endurance.

Nevine's resolution not to spend her remaining years alone

wasn't trivial. She knew she would die, but not soon. It took many tries before she could tear off the vines of loneliness, which began by constricting her breathing and ended by giving her the crushing sensation that nothing else lay in store for her. She woke alone every morning, unconcerned with the preoccupations shared by the rest of mankind. Nevine no longer thought of being a grandmother; that dream was over, and now she was suspended in space. She wouldn't reconsider her break with her husband's family; her absurd battle with them for influence had wasted enough time already. She'd spent years embroiled in gratuitous conflicts whose triviality she felt only now. Everything she had built was destroyed—the family, the house—the only thing she could do now was wait to die, but death remained such a distant prospect, in her mind. Victory in the revolution meant nothing to her anymore, other than the chance of seeing her son's murderers dragged through the streets. She was gripped by fantasies of revenge for losses for which there was no possible restitution. After losing their compassion, a person becomes little more than another corpse abandoned by the roadside, one that should really be buried. She knew that she was already just such a body, but she still needed to die before she could find peace under the earth. And for her, dying was the hardest work of all.

A year after her marriage to Abdel Latif, Nevine's feelings had changed. She no longer felt she was waiting to die, and she no longer wanted to stay in S, but then she couldn't let herself move away from her son's grave. She didn't like living so close to the dead, but whenever she thought about leaving, she felt paralyzed—her legs went numb. Sometimes she felt a great yearning for the gossip and fleeting quarrels with her former sisters-in-law, who once tried to intervene in her life, but all that was finished. They had always been haughty women, convinced they belonged to such a powerful family; now, they were migrants in refugee camps, expecting sympathy. They had lost everything: their houses, their children, and their lives of plenty.

As he listened to his father go on and on about Nevine, his town, and his revolution, Bolbol could only assume that he was making it all up. It wasn't possible for a man in his seventies and a woman over sixty, the mother of two martyrs, no less, to chase through meadows after butterflies and write each other love letters as if they were separated by a great distance; equally, it was impossible to sit in the sights of a never-ending military bombardment and yet spend hours talking about the moon. But, then again, he could hardly call his father a liar.

In those moments, Abdel Latif had wanted to tell Bolbol that he was no longer a lonely old man in need of care; he hadn't been toppled; he had regained his former vitality, and all at once. He reflected on his life without anger, he entertained no illusions, nor did he let himself get carried away. In this, father and son were much alike: Bolbol understood the truth of his own life, too, in those days—that he had changed considerably, and that the solitude whose merits he discussed with Abdel Latif wasn't so terrible. He still remembered how his name had changed from Nabil to Bolbol; Lamia began to call him Bolbol as a pet name, and in the early days of his solitary life he had liked hearing others use the same name that Lamia used. His original name was almost completely forgotten at this point. Whenever Bolbol saw it on official documents, he felt it belonged to someone else. "Bolbol" sounded lighter and more human to him, whereas "Nabil" suggested some well-adjusted man still dreaming of a grand future. Recently, Bolbol had lost even the impulse to dream and make plans; carrying out his father's last wish was an exercise of what little remained of his will. After all, you have to do *something* if you aren't just going to lie down and die—if you don't want to sink down to the center of the earth.

The corpse swaying to and fro in the minibus was the only truth he had left. He still thought of it as a real person, a collection of tangible, worldly sensations: it could do things; it wasn't just a gelatinous lump. It had a family, and that family still had a long way to go, and on the journey maybe they might even talk like real siblings again.

They traveled fifty kilometers in four hours. Agents at three checkpoints were relatively patient with the family when they saw the bloated body. The third checkpoint allowed them to pass using the lane reserved for military use only, and hope was revived that they might reach Anabiya before evening. Along the road, the signs of battles were clearly visible: damaged tanks, burned-out cars, dried bloodstains. The houses by the road were destroyed and abandoned, and other houses in the distance seemed to have been scorched. Very few people and animals moved through the streets of the small semi-abandoned villages; the only visible morning activities were death and exodus. A double-cab pickup passed them on the road, filled with soldiers armed to the teeth. They flagged down the minibus and the other cars and ordered them to stop and clear the road for a line of tanks. The people in the stopped cars avoided looking at the long convoy. Hussein approached a car driven by a man in his sixties, traveling with his wife and a daughter, who looked around thirteen. A Pullman coach stopped behind them, taking passengers to Aleppo, some of whom got out to smoke. Hussein joined them to chat, waving his hand at Bolbol and Fatima and nodding along with whatever the passengers were saying. It was the very picture of people brought together by tragedy, far from home, trying to dismiss their fear by making small talk.

The tank convoy was still passing when planes swooped overhead. The drivers and their passengers watched the planes bomb some place invisible from this vantage point, and the sound those bombs made gave the strong impression that death was even more imminent than usual. The line of vehicles and their marooned passengers reflected that it was useless to try to resist death. Everyone surrendered to what was to come; no one thought of running away. Where would they go? Hussein came back to the minibus as everyone tried to stick together or else find somewhere to hide; very few were still wandering around bored and smoking. The minutes of horror eventually passed, the airplanes left, and silence descended on the vast wilderness. The final military vehicle accompanying the line of tanks signaled that it was all right for the civilians to continue, so long as none of them overtook the convoy.

It was now almost one o'clock; reaching Anabiya before sunset again seemed a lost cause. Most of the idling cars pulled out all at once; of course, every one of the travelers wanted to reach their destinations before nightfall. After five kilometers, however, they all had to stop again; the cars that had tried to overtake the rest reappeared, and their drivers signaled to everyone that they couldn't go forward. Volleys of bullets could be heard nearby, behind a hill only a few kilometers away.

Bolbol considered their predicament. Once again, where would they go? There was nowhere but here, out in the open. They stopped the minibus by one of the big passenger coaches, and some other cars stopped close to them. They all stood there for an hour or two. Then the sound of gunfire stopped, and news passed among the vehicles that a battalion of guerrillas had attacked the line of tanks and had now retreated to their original positions. The tanks had been diverted onto the military road leading to the villages south of Aleppo. Six tanks from the convoy were burned out; one of them contained the remnants of a dead man that his comrades had left as food for wild animals.

It was the only corpse visible. Smoke was still rising from the rest of the destroyed tanks. Bolbol thought of this body and dreaded Hussein seeing it, in case it led him to play that same old broken record he'd been spinning since they left home: that bodies weren't important in war, loved ones could make do with a torn shirt or a severed leg wrapped in a shroud inside a closed coffin . . . Many families had buried their loved ones without once laying eyes on the horrifying sight of their dismembered corpses.

Bolbol knew that if his father weren't a cadaver, he would be going on and on about all the features of the area. He would be telling his children the names of the local villages, would be listing the flora and fauna, the produce the region was famed for, even its precise elevation above sea level. It had been his favorite hobby, to explain the geography of each district he passed through, but a corpse couldn't do any of that.

Evening began to fall. Reaching Anabiya before midnight was out of the question. Bolbol convinced himself that everything would be easy once they reached Aleppo; only forty kilometers separated Aleppo and Anabiya, and they would travel that distance easily, especially as they were from the area and belonged to a well-known family. His father, who had fled his family more than forty-five years earlier, would nonetheless be saved by its name. Bolbol shared his optimism with Hussein and Fatima, but was discomfited by their silence. Hussein was wondering despairingly, *But when will we reach Aleppo?* Fatima's frightened face made it plain to the others that their predicament, stuck on a half-impassable road crossing abandoned villages and boundless wilderness, wouldn't be an easy one to escape. Hussein was now convinced that patience was the only thing that might save them, and he no longer suggested burying the body by the side of the road or in one of the graveyards belonging to these small villages. (He had pointed out that they could always come back after a time to retrieve it—no one would steal a stranger's body—but, then, bodies won't wait: they soon rot and melt into the earth.)

The siblings tried to limit conversation and made monosyllabic replies to any questions. All three were thinking how they would need to work together as a family in order to get their father's body to its last resting place; all were thinking about how they would return to their loneliness and isolation after the burial, how they would have to avoid looking into one another's eyes for fear of discovering the extent of the gulf separating them. The blissful days of their childhood, when they would exchange secrets, when they could still believe that their life was happy and full of ease, were well and truly over. What had happened couldn't be explained, but they were no longer anything like their childhood selves. Hussein more than either of the others was a stranger to his original character; Fatima and Bolbol, like their father before them, couldn't believe he had changed so much. He was no longer a smart, ambitious, strong young man but had become an entirely different person. Anyone who didn't know him would think he was going out of his way to get himself killed.

Hussein had been closest to the siblings' parents and was the most spoiled. He won all the prizes at school and captained the soccer team to unimaginable victories all around and outside Damascus before returning borne aloft on his classmates' shoulders. He would lead his friends on crazy adventures in the alleys of Bab Tuma, where they would skulk and make dates with girls, spending hours in those cafés that allowed teenagers to press against and fondle one another in darkened corners. He invented lies for the benefit of their credulous families and took these girls on long trips to the meadows of Ghouta to woo them with his guitar to the songs of Muhammad Jamal and Sabah before spiriting his beloveds away behind some nearby trees where they would exchange long kisses and he would touch their breasts. He encouraged all his friends to be reckless and take chances. He kept their secrets and passed a terrible judgment on anyone who broke their word. All the girls trusted him and asked him to help them solve their romantic problems—this or that teenage drama, such as someone threatening to shame his girlfriend by sending some rather personal pictures to her family after a fight. Hussein would intervene forcefully, put a stop to the threat, speak to the boyfriend as though he were the girl's brother, and that was usually the end of the matter. The muscles he was beginning to build up from sports helped him to make credible threats, and he emerged victorious from the many fights he waded into.

Everything changed for Hussein when he reached high school: by that time he was no longer an idealistic boy, but had grown strong and athletic. A woman in her thirties fell in love with him, and within a few months she had transformed him into her bodyguard, escorting her on mysterious errands. He stayed with her for days at a time in the apartment she rented that overlooked the Mezzeh highway and he would return exhausted from being kept up all night. He wouldn't brook any discussion with his father; when he was bombarded with questions, he packed a suitcase and left for weeks, and no one in his family knew where he'd gone.

Hussein left school before finishing his high-school degree and settled happily into his new life. The night of their big fight, he was insolent to the father who was only trying to help him. After calmly telling him that they had to speak as equals, Hussein explained, in blunt language, that he had no desire to repeat his father's small-town life of teaching and respectability. He said he hated the world of weaklings; he wanted to live among the powerful. He would creep into their lives and become one of them; he would share their wealth, sleep with beautiful women, travel to different countries, and live in a mansion in the richest part of town.

His father proceeded cautiously in this discussion. He explained the concept of strength of mind, but was mired in customs and traditions that couldn't convince his son. As for Hussein, he spoke harsh truths that couldn't be denied. He pointed out Abdel Latif was the most highly regarded geography teacher in the school, and even so his meager salary alone couldn't keep the family afloat for two whole weeks. His wife was forced to earn a paltry sum shelling peas and beans and peeling garlic for the grocery stores in the rich parts of town. Hussein added coolly that he didn't want his wife to peel garlic and chop vegetables for rich women in exchange for a few pennies.

Hussein went on. He told his father quietly that Abdel Latif might know all about Brazil and the topography of the Alps, but he didn't know what went on in his neighbors' houses. He didn't know that in this utopia, families sold their daughters to rich Arab tourists who demanded some enjoyment while passing through (of course, legitimized by a temporary marriage contract), and he didn't know that women who worked in the civil service would go out with men in exchange for a pair of shoes, and they didn't have to be expensive ones. His father choked at this and no longer knew how to defend his way of life. He stood accused, along with all the sons of his generation, of the fear and cowardice that had brought his country to the point where it was willing to sell its daughters.

This sort of talk was unheard of in Abdel Latif's house. In the silence following Hussein's tirade, he wondered if his father might not die of shock that very moment. Abdel Latif couldn't believe that this was his son, not yet nineteen—a young man caring nothing for the values his father prized above everything else: honor and integrity and morality. Before Hussein got sluggishly to his feet and left the house, he declared these values worth no more than his mother's plastic slippers and suggested his father accompany him for a few days to see the real marvels of the city. But Abdel Latif had long since refused to ride in Hussein's car, a Golf 1976 that his lover had bought to make it easier for him to accompany her and her friends on their private errands. His clients weren't stingy when it came to encouraging Hussein to fulfill their special requests—an extra pinch of hashish or a few grams of cocaine—with alacrity; besides, all Hussein really ever wanted was enough cash for dinner in a restaurant in Bloudan with a girl who was wearing only a skimpy negligee under her coat.

Abdel Latif managed one last sentence. He told Hussein that he couldn't be both a pimp and his son. Hussein took exception to the word "pimp." He took out his identity card and scratched out his father's name: "I'll write 'shit' in its place," he said as he stormed out, leaving nothing but confusion in his wake.

None of Hussein's family saw him for two years after that. Abdel Latif forbade anyone from mentioning his name. He judged what had happened to be reason enough to consider his son dead. Sometime later, a woman who didn't give her name called to inform them that their son was an inmate at Adra Prison, something to do with drugs.

Hussein, who had been his father's pride and joy, had become his shame, and Bolbol was no good as a replacement: his weakness and anxiety had never exactly endeared him to Abdel Latif. This didn't especially bother Bolbol. No one ever bets on the weak. Strength of mind, that quality of which his father used to speak so highly, was Bolbol's only departure from the weakness that otherwise seemed to define his character, but the fact was that Abdel Latif had only really valued Hussein's physical strength and refused to lay a wager on Bolbol's mind. Bolbol was happy to be overlooked; he didn't want to be a racehorse, and he didn't have the energy to realize the dreams of a family that struck him as not only defeated, but one whose defeat only grew larger with each passing day—larger in every heart and in every corner of their home.

Hussein's cruel words shocked them with facts they had been doing their best to avoid. They had been living in this small town for many years, but they were still outsiders. Despite their perpetual belief that they weren't poor, in truth they were not at all well off, as most families working in the public sector weren't. Everything around them, everything their father had built, Hussein turned to rubble in seconds. Their father hadn't had the courage to live in Damascus, for fear of getting lost; he liked gatherings where everyone was somehow linked by familial or party ties. He couldn't bear the thought of being a stranger in a large city, but in the end he'd still become the stranger he had never wanted to be. At first, whenever Abdel Latif was mentioned by a native of S, they reiterated his connection to Anabiya: it wasn't easy to escape that identity, but even this would pass in time. Returning to Anabiya was no longer feasible. It seemed very far away; as if all his friends had died or had forgotten their childhood, or indeed anything that linked them with Abdel Latif as members of the same generation.

After Hussein left the house, their father was silent for three days. He didn't leave his room and ate only a few morsels. His wife was indifferent to the behavior of both. Bolbol soon thought it might be a good idea for him to get away for a while himself; Abdel Latif wouldn't be able to get past what had happened as long as he knew Bolbol, his other son, who had witnessed everything, was around. Bolbol asked permission to travel to Anabiya, as he did every year, to spend a few days with his kindhearted aunt Amina—a good way to keep himself from being underfoot. He told his mother, "I'll be back in a week, and everything will be fine again."

His grandfather's house in Anabiya was long gone. There was only a collection of relatives left there, most of whom had forgotten some time ago that Bolbol's family ever existed, particularly after Abdel Latif refused to participate in their various and venerable family feuds, which he considered a backward practice for the latter half of the twentieth century. Only Aunt Amina had continued to care. On Bolbol's visits she would tell him their family history, and he would try to piece together the story of his father's flight from his village and his family. The story his aunt always told had parts missing, and she stopped at the first mention of the three knights, as they were known in the village: Abdel Latif and his cousins, Jamil and Abdel Karim. They were the first young men in the village to get their high-school diplomas, tramping the muddy winter lanes half barefoot to reach the school in Afrin, which in the early sixties was still a small, clean town. It required the strength of a mule to make that journey every morning and to return every night. Beneath the pouring rain, the three would cross the fields on foot, sometimes sleeping at a friend's house or in a mosque when floods closed the road. They couldn't afford to rent a small room in town, and their determination to finish school forced their families to save small amounts to cover their fees.

Abdel Latif would boast of how they lived: the whole winter they would cook lentil soup and bulgur wheat and walk barefoot to school; they would distribute Baath Party leaflets and get thrown in jail; they would face the whip and still hold out. Knowledge was a battle and politics a sacrifice, as well as a contest, he would conclude to his audience, who had heard the tale hundreds of times. No one in Anabiya remembered those battles now, but they certainly didn't forget Bolbol's uncle, Lieutenant Colonel Jamil, who, if he'd had better luck, might have wound up president of the republic. As it was he had been betrayed by certain friends who'd slandered him and his associates. As the price for their defamatory comments, those men had accepted an amount of influence that still wasn't exhausted forty years later. Everything was upside down, now: the whole family was branded as traitors, and the slanderers were considered heroes.

The corpse of Abdel Latif, now laid out on a minibus seat, gave no indication of the man's past strength of conviction—that Palestine would one day be fully liberated, for example, and that he would one day pray with his friends in al-Aqsa Mosque. Forty years earlier Abdel Latif had picked up his tin suitcase and left his village for good, after he had failed to support his sister Layla in her refusal to marry a man she didn't love. Not even when she said, "I'll set myself on fire before I marry a man who stinks of rotten onions." And, sure enough, on the day of the wedding she had been forced into, she stood on the roof of her family's tall house in her white dress, poured out a jug of kerosene, and set herself alight, carrying out the threat no one had taken seriously. She whirled around like a Sufi to best let the flames take her body, which had become a charred corpse before anyone could reach her. Abdel Latif had watched her from a distance, weeping for her silently, as his three children were doing now for him: despite how bad life had become, death could still seem terribly cruel.

Yes, as the minibus traveled on, the three siblings preferred to focus on memories and stories rather than think about being stuck on this journey. Bolbol said to himself, If I'd seen even half of this coming, I would have buried him anywhere there was space . . . Taking his father's body to his friends in S would have been easier by far. They had fallen into Abdel Latif's trap. As well as their burden his body was now their only means of escape—because it did still stir up some sympathy, sometimes, and it was the only justification they could point to for their being together on the road at such a time.

They were delighted when the next checkpoint showed them a little compassion. Bolbol reflected that in war, little things like that were enough to give you hope: a considerate soldier at a checkpoint, a checkpoint without traffic, a bomb falling a hundred meters away from you on a car that had cut you off and taken your turn in line . . . *Chance has just given us a new life! If that car hadn't shown up, the bomb would have fallen on us!* This is how people think when even their highest hopes have been brought so low to the ground. The happiness of being able to end your journey at last completely overwhelms your sadness for the victims when you see their charred remains as you pass their car. You need to set aside your compassion so you don't wind up facing yourself and acknowledging the bitter truth: in the face of a meaningless death, hanging on to the self becomes a task as sacred as it is selfish. Over the past twelve hundred days, Bolbol had often reflected on the numerous coincidences that had saved his life. He even began to act as though fate had taken a special interest in him; when somebody panicked and pushed past him onto a bus, he told himself that being forced to take a later bus was no doubt for the best. The first bus was probably going to be hit by a bomb or maybe get caught up in a sudden firefight. Death passes by, and you can't grasp it. In war, death is blind. It never stops to look at its victims.

For the first time, it occurred to Bolbol that the road, with all its rituals and its twists and turns, resembled the people who traveled on it: In the early morning, the dew-laden trees in the distance and the moist earth on either side of the minibus had filled him with optimism. By the afternoon, however, he was exhausted. The changeable weather was damper than usual; storms would blow up and then subside. The three passengers were focused entirely on arriving; they couldn't bear enduring the body's company for another night. It had begun to rot in earnest now, and the cologne, which Fatima desperately sprinkled over it every few minutes, no longer helped.

Hussein seemed calm now. It helped Bolbol and Fatima to relax. They once again postponed the exchange of accusations they had each been nurturing. Bolbol stood the most accused, of course, for having embroiled everyone in this hellish journey they were no longer sure would ever end. The bravery they had boasted of had turned into a nightmare; the moment of their decision now seemed one of insane recklessness, but, even so, a secret satisfaction was creeping into Bolbol. He was no longer the person he had been for four years. He wished he could go back to the beginning, as he was now, so he could spit in his petty neighbors' faces for perpetually spying on him and never trusting him.

He began to understand the secret of his father's regained

strength late in life: his psychic wounds all healing at once, his attitude changing, his no longer acting like a rotten fish waiting to be thrown into the nearest gutter. His eyes got back their twinkle; his body seemed to regain its youthful elegance; he started shaving again; he wore his new favorite clothes. Like a young man he exchanged his threadbare suits for jeans, T-shirts, and sneakers to help him outrun sniper fire. He didn't sit and wait for the protests to pass his house but went to the mosque two hours before the afternoon prayer. He had never prayed in his life—everyone knew he was there to wait for the protests. He spoke with the young people and ignored their pleas to wait for them in front of his house where the protest passed every Friday. He thought up slogans and discussed new ideas. He reread the histories of revolutions and underlined many sentences. He offered copious explanations of the greatest revolutions in history, and his abundant enthusiasm made him into an icon. He resumed his role in the town as the respected teacher who was still fondly remembered by his students, and he lived the bitterness and the glory of the revolution alongside them. When Bolbol met up with his father for the penultimate time, he saw that Abdel Latif was no longer an old man filled with bitterness and loss, just waiting to die; he was an active man whose telephone rang at all hours, who had high hopes of living to see the regime fall and breathing in the freedom for which he had waited for so long.

In early May 2011, Bolbol found Lamia knocking at his door unexpectedly. Her eyes blazed, and she said, "There's no time to lose, we're going to S." Without waiting for a reply, she went on to say she was joining the protests that day. Bolbol couldn't get out of it, and they arrived at ten o'clock in the morning. She hugged Abdel Latif and embarked on a strange conversation with him about their moribund town, which expected sparks to fly today.

Bolbol instantly resumed his other personality, the reckless, impulsive one that Lamia believed in, and went out with them. He was afraid, but when they blended with the huge crowd he could pretend he had broken with his former life, at least for the time being; peculiar feelings struck him and he shouted defiantly. His voice was weak at first, almost mute in contrast to his father's and Lamia's, who raised their hands in the air, their voices as strong as the other twenty thousand people shouting at once. Their voices rocked the town, whose entrances were being guarded by young men observing the road. They signaled to the other protesters when they spotted vehicles carrying soldiers approaching the town. After half an hour Bolbol merged with the others and truly began to shout. He felt a vehement delight; the moment he buried his fear was like his first orgasm. He tried to regain that feeling several times; although he couldn't return to it, he could never forget it. It was an incomplete, unrepeatable pleasure, and it remained suspended in his life like the pendulum of a clock. More than twenty cars bristling with Mukhabarat and machine guns charged the protest and opened fire at close range. Bolbol saw bodies fall in a horrifying scene. Lamia, prostrate on the ground, was helped up by a young man who took her arm and escaped with her into a narrow alley. They were close to his father's house, but Abdel Latif wouldn't budge; he wanted to accept his own portion of death. Dead bodies were strewn everywhere. The Mukhabarat retreated after less than an hour—but that was more than enough time for a massacre. When Bolbol reached his father's house, Lamia was waiting for him. She asked about his father, and he told her he had left Abdel Latif standing there, waiting for a merciful bullet. Again, the sound of gunfire broke out, and they heard young people running and cursing the regime and the Mukhabarat. Lamia opened the door when she saw that the neighbors had all done the same—letting the protesters seek shelter in their houses.

It was a great day. His father relived it a thousand times. As for Bolbol, that one visit was enough for him. Lamia stopped knocking on his door in the morning to take him with her to his father's house.

She told him she felt an affinity with the martyrs who had fallen that day. She'd spent that night in Abdel Latif's house, and they'd both helped to treat the wounded over at Nevine's larger house, which had been turned into a field hospital. The town didn't sleep; the families of the fallen kept vigil by the bodies of their sons and daughters. The army and the Mukhabarat patrols made relentless house raids and arrested scores of young people. Bolbol stayed alone in his father's house. Abdel Latif and Lamia didn't return before dawn. Bolbol heard them talking about the wounded by name. He tossed and turned, but didn't get up. Lamia slept in Fatima's room. Before she and Abdel Latif went to sleep, Bolbol heard his father ask her to wake him in the morning so they could go to the funerals.

Come morning, Bolbol didn't dare flee, afraid that Lamia would think he was a coward. He tried to think of something that would cheer her up, and so prepared a large breakfast, but she and his father ate only a few mouthfuls and drank a few sips of coffee before they left to go back to the field hospital. Loudspeakers at the mosque were inviting people to attend the funerals after the after-noon prayer; public defiance was at its height. Bolbol wondered if fear might finally have changed sides; Lamia told him that she had seen soldiers looking terrified the moment they opened fire on unarmed people. But no, Bolbol told himself, this was artistic license, nothing more. How could someone holding a weapon be frightened by unarmed people waving nothing but their bare hands? Yet her innocent eyes seemed to tell him that lies and exaggeration were simply foreign to Lamia; on the contrary, she was always humble in her estimation of herself, deferring to others and overvaluing their roles in her life. Often, she had made Bolbol feel he was very important to her, asking him to do small favors and thanking him profusely afterward. She was the type who considered the presence of others to be a reward in itself. Bolbol was relieved when Lamia and his father didn't ask him to accompany them to the field hospital. He went back to bed. He was still there when the funeral procession approached the house; curiosity prevented him from going back to sleep. He climbed to the roof and saw a flood of people below. Women were performing *zagharid*, ululating triumphantly, and roses and rice were being thrown from balconies. His father climbed the steps to the church with Father Walim; they grasped the rope of the huge bell and tolled it with all their strength while twenty thousand people raised their fists in the air in reply. It was an awe-inspiring scene, and Bolbol didn't notice the tears slipping down his own cheeks.

Lamia was in the middle of the crowd, weeping and shouting; even where he stood on the roof, he could tell that her voice was screamed almost raw. The funeral procession passed, and a few minutes later Bolbol heard the sound of gunfire. Six young men and a woman were killed close to where Lamia stood; she spent the night delirious, her mind refusing to grasp what had happened. Bolbol's fear returned and increased; he felt as though he personally were under siege. His father paced the living room furiously and spoke on the phone to his friend Nadir, a math teacher, telling him he would meet him at the graveyard. He hung up and left in a hurry. Bolbol followed him with a recklessness he hadn't thought himself capable of, but then he, too, was furious.

Lamia wouldn't listen when his father said that women shouldn't attend the burial. She followed them, and all three hurried to the graveyard. The streets of S were deserted, and the smell of death wafted through the houses and alleys. The electricity had been cut off, and they were all enveloped in darkness. As they went through the narrow alleys, men were preparing to pray over the bodies. Lamia headed toward a group of women, relatives of the dead. Bolbol sat on a tombstone and watched from a distance. His childhood friends kissed him hastily in greeting and continued to where the men were completing the burial rites. The faces of the martyrs gleamed in the light of the full moon.

Lamia was still filled with rage as they left S. She cursed the regime with a wide variety of obscenities while Bolbol kept quiet, unsure how to make her feel better. She left him suddenly in the neighborhood of Baramkeh. She kissed him affectionately and hailed a taxi to take her to the bus depot, and then Bolbol was suddenly alone in the middle of the traffic, a small rabbit in a sea of people. The faces of the crowds around him were impassive, and he panted for deliverance.

Now Bolbol was staring outside the minibus, switching from one side of the road to the other. If this nightmare ever ended, and they ever reached Anabiya, he would wash his hands of the past entirely. He no longer had a father or a mother, and all links to his siblings would be severed for good. He would insist that his own son bury him in the nearest possible graveyard. He didn't want anyone to read the Fatiha over his grave; what good did that do the dead? Everything the living did for the dead just highlighted the solitude of the dead and satisfied the vanity of the living; all that chatter in remembrance of a dead person's good qualities was nothing more than jockeying for social position. Few would have objected if the three siblings had tossed their father's body into a ditch, but perhaps they, too, were taking risks only in order to win admiring glances from their friends and neighbors. Those looks hadn't meant much to them before, but now they could see themselves being consumed by the supposed nobility of their task. If they succumbed to such vanity, they could easily wind up joining the ranks of the self-righteous, those people who consider themselves worthy of passing judgment on everyone who can't live up to their own high moral standards—a group united only by its isolation.

By now they were pessimistic about ever reaching Anabiya at all. Bolbol had switched roles with Hussein, who had taken on the role of the sensible older brother, praising his father and trying to keep Bolbol and Fatima calm. At the ninth checkpoint, the guards were actually kind to them. They told them to hurry if they wanted to reach Anabiya before midnight and pointed out where the next checkpoint would be. They said it belonged to the security services and advised the siblings to answer any questions briefly and without any obstruction; the agents manning that station were miserable, as they hadn't been on leave in months. The siblings prepared themselves, and Bolbol left it to Hussein to decide whether to take the lane for goods or for passengers. Hussein stopped a few meters before the start of the bottleneck at the checkpoint and hurried to the officer in charge. He explained their situation and asked to be allowed to pass in view of their special circumstances, mentioning that the body had begun to rot. The officer came with him to the minibus and glanced at the corpse. He ordered them to go into the goods lane and kept hold of their documents. Hussein said, "When we get to the Free Army territory, everything will be easier. Our identity cards will help us to cross checkpoints quickly." Fatima closed her eyes and murmured a prayer; it occurred to Bolbol, as he looked at her, that this journey had turned her into an old woman. Despair had crept into her heart. He said to Hussein that they still had a little money left, which might speed up their passage through the checkpoint and help them get their identity cards back. Hussein pointed coolly outside. They were trapped inside a lane closed off by huge cement blocks and couldn't leave until all the cars in front of them had passed through; money wouldn't do a thing.

Cars on the other side of the barrier were asking Hussein about the road ahead, and he replied wryly, "There's always someone who knows the road, and everyone follows him." A man who opened his car window was taken aback when Hussein yelled to him without warning that they were carrying a corpse, which was why they were in the goods lane. The man tried to avoid looking at them and continued his conversation with his corpulent wife, who watched them out of the corner of her eye. In a wave of black glee, Hussein asked the driver of another small car for an aspirin because the stink of the corpse had given him a headache. The man just fiddled with his steering wheel without replying to Hussein, who said to his siblings, "We have to have some fun. In a few hours we'll all be dead of cold, or of the smell." He turned up the volume of his tape player a little and began to drum out the rhythm of the songs. Fatima glared at him, but Hussein didn't care. Bolbol prayed to all the gods that their task would end successfully, with everyone still sane. No one could predict Hussein's reactions now, and Bolbol couldn't complete the journey by himself. He needed Hussein to be in his right mind; he was more than familiar with this other face of his, which sneered at everything. Life had wounded him deeply; he had lost all his dreams, and his present was nothing but a nihilistic wait for nothing in particular. He would always be a private driver for a group of Russian dancers working in a club in

Damascus, waiting outside their cheap hotel to convey them to the cabaret, coming back at four in the morning to bring them home again. His life had become one long errand. By day he worked as a minibus driver just to get out of his house.

It wasn't for this that Hussein had broken with Abdel Latif. He'd dreamed of leading an empire, not of becoming a petty driver for a bunch of women who sometimes ordered him to pull over and negotiate with potential clients on their behalf. In those moments he felt like a disgusting insect or, as his father put it, a cheap pimp. He worked for free for a small, obscure gang that sold things on behalf of a large, well-known gang. They were connected to the Mukhabarat and worked openly to sell Russian escorts, hashish, cocaine, and heroin. But he was on the lowest level in this gang, with no hope of ascending to become a full member. Everything was finished, in his opinion. He was no good for anything anymore.

Hussein, persisting in his drumming, switched to the radio and began to sing along loudly to the Saria Sawas song playing. The solemnity and dignity of the presence of death was dispelled. Fatima looked at Bolbol, hoping perhaps that he would reestablish order. For his part, Bolbol was amused by what he saw and wished he could join in the singing; such futility could only be defeated by song and laughter. Often, he had seen people sitting silent and despondent at an *'aza*, avoiding one another's gazes so they wouldn't burst out laughing and ruin the mourning.

They would be waiting a long time if things carried on this slowly. The agents at the checkpoint were scrutinizing everything: identity cards, bags, cups. They examined the cars carefully, shooting out unexpected questions about the passengers' occupations and intended destinations, questions that were normal in themselves but disconcerting when asked by an armed group of men more like a mob than an official squadron. They stood at the check-points with their fingers on their triggers. Their clothes and head-scarves denoted sectarian affiliations; Hezbollah badges mixed with the green badges of the Iraqi Shi'ite groups who were working with the death squads established by the regime. There were no curbs on their behavior; they were entitled to pass judgment on any person for any infringement, execute them, and throw them in a mass grave, or else just leave them where they fell for their family to pick up and take away.

After an hour and a half of waiting, the minibus pulled up to the checkpoint proper. The three siblings didn't speak until spo-ken to. The bearded agent who poked his head into the van was as-tonished at the body. Hussein explained everything in a defeated tone, seeking a little more sympathy on account of the rapidly dis-integrating corpse. Abdel Latif's tissues had slackened, and his pores had fissured; his lower half had turned blue, his stomach had inflated, and the stench was overpowering. The agent asked them to pull over on the right and get out of the vehicle. Half an hour later they were a pitiful sight; Fatima was trembling with cold, and Hussein wore an unusually imploring look. No one spoke to them or asked any questions. This limbo of waiting could be so perilous; sometimes, soldiers would drag young men off the buses and spirit them away into nearby buildings before allowing the vehicles to pass through.

Of course, this checkpoint, like so many others, seemed less like a proper checkpoint than a small barracks surrounded by tanks. A short improvised tower was positioned on the barracks roof with snipers stationed inside, observing everyone, perpetually ready to kill. There was thunder in the air, and suddenly it was no longer distant thunder but right on top of them. The storm was approaching, but time was crawling by as usual. Bolbol found himself imagining his family stuck in place for a whole day, or a whole week. It was becoming impossible to believe that their father's body merited such risk and sacrifice, that it should be treated so respectfully, when death reaped hundreds every day throughout the length and breadth of the country. Who could possibly make such an argument now?

Bolbol exchanged a glance with Hussein that they both understood. Bolbol approached another agent guarding the checkpoint who was smoking calmly and tried to explain their situation to him. They needed to reach Anabiya before midnight in order to be rid of the pestilential corpse. The agent referred him back to the officer inside the building, adding that they couldn't pass without his permission. The corpse had become an object of revulsion without an identity; it wasn't merchandise and it wasn't a person. After death a person becomes a third sort of thing, neither animal nor mineral. Records are closed on their account; they are struck out of the family ledgers with a red line; their belongings are thrown into garbage bags or picked over by scavengers from near and far. No one asks old bedsheets about the warmth of the bodies they once protected in the heat of passion. After the file is closed on a dead person, all these little details are shed piece by piece by the memories of the living. Everything is consigned to oblivion and nothingness.

Bolbol went to the officer in charge with an attitude of supplication. In a trembling voice, he explained that time was of the essence; he spoke about the dignity of the dead, not mentioning that they were stuck with this corpse if they couldn't reach Anabiya. He made himself look wretched, begging without complaining. He hated how naturally the pose came to him; a brave man would say something different, would affirm his right to move about freely and take his father's body to its graveyard in good time . . .

The officer looked at Bolbol coldly, used to the blandishments of those who had fallen inside his trap. As far as he was concerned, all these people hated him and wouldn't have any mercy if their situations were reversed. The roles of executioner and victim were eternally being exchanged, were they not?

Bolbol thought of the pouring rain and raging storm outside. Night would fall soon, and they wouldn't be able to finish their journey in this weather. The officer said that transporting bodies in this fashion was forbidden, but because he believed that they were acting without malice, he was waiting for confirmation of the death certificate. Bolbol offered to try and get the pronouncing doctor on his cell phone, but the man in charge cut him off sharply: "Life and death are only a matter of official documents." He pointed at the fax machine on his desk. Bolbol asked permission, again, to call someone at the hospital who might be able to expedite matters, and the officer nodded his acquiescence. Bolbol dialed the doctor's number and explained the problem to him. The doctor promised to look for the fax from the checkpoint and to get back to them as quickly as possible.

Bolbol had almost no money left; he blamed himself for having wasted it, for not having properly calculated the cost of their long journey: he should have divided the sum between the total number of anticipated checkpoints. They had nothing they could sell here—Bolbol's phone was ancient and wouldn't fetch more than a thousand liras, while Hussein would never relinquish his phone for any price—and the two thousand liras left in the siblings' collective possession wouldn't get them anything. The doctor called back and told Bolbol that the hospital's fax machine had been out of order for three months. Only then did Bolbol remember Fatima's ring and wondered how much it might fetch. He went back out into the driving rain and explained the situation to Hussein and Fatima, who were huddled in the minibus for shelter, but still soaked right through. Fatima had slipped her feet under the blanket that served as their father's shroud. Hussein explained that he couldn't turn on the heat; they needed to save gas.

They all looked at one another, acknowledging that they were lost in the wilderness, until an agent rapped on the bus's window and gestured at Bolbol to get back out. The agent returned the documents to him and said that a fax had arrived from the hospital; the officer was allowing them to proceed. They couldn't believe they were being allowed to go on their way. The minibus set off, and Hussein put as much distance as he could between themselves and the checkpoint. He regained his good spirits, and Fatima muttered strange litanies and asked him to look through his cassette tapes for a prayer for traveling. Hussein didn't reply; he was busy speaking to one of his friends on the phone, telling him the name of the village they'd passed through a few minutes earlier. His friend told him there were still ten kilometers until they reached the final regime checkpoint. After that, they would enter the territory of the Free Syrian Army. Hussein focused on the road. The rain stopped, but the wind picked up speed; it tilted the minibus, and the corpse began to topple. Bolbol grabbed it before it could fall over and considered laying it flat on the floor. He dismissed the idea, however; to move it would be to risk revealing even more of its decay. They did their best to ignore the stink, though they were on the brink of passing out: the cologne mixed with the corpse's odor weighed the air with a putrid, lethal stench, and the biting cold outside prevented them from opening any windows.

Each sibling was too ashamed now to admit that they regretted ever setting out on this journey. Why hadn't they looked for a more convenient graveyard, or maybe called one of those charities that volunteered to finance burials for strangers to the city?

Their silence also made it clear just how little they could stand spending so much time with one another. An entire day was intolerable; there was nothing left in them of the affectionate siblings of old. The ties of blood simply weren't enough to sustain the falsehood of family harmony given all the things that now divided them—a lie that in any case had disintegrated long before. When Hussein told their father what they were all thinking, back then, he paid the price of his recklessness; Bolbol meanwhile kept trying to live the lie of respect and the sacred family bond. There were many times he would have liked to tell his father that he was cruel to his children and kind only to his students and strangers. The image Abdel Latif presented to the world was paramount; he cared too much about what people said about him and believed only the best of what they said. He didn't respect his children's weaknesses because he didn't remember his own, nor his old inability to escape with Layla from his own family's influence. He had waited for her to turn to ash before he let out a stifled cry and left Anabiya for good—Anabiya, where now he wanted to be buried. Bolbol wanted to ask him: *Why, after you left it all behind—those cruel faces that knew no mercy—why would you want to be buried on their cursed land?*

It wasn't the first time he had pictured himself standing in front of his father, speechifying to him, telling him to his face that he was a weak, emasculated man with barely a quarter of a dream to brag of, which wasn't nearly enough to achieve anything effective. His tirade would conclude: *You're like me, but you wrap your delu-*

sions in big words about the liberation of Palestine, which your gen-eration left to rot. Or maybe something about the respectable family Abdel Latif had always wanted, filled with successful, educated, socialist children working in respectable professions: *Like all poor people you want your children to become doctors or engineers, but your uniqueness is a fantasy and the cost of it has buried us.*

When Bolbol decided to study philosophy, he felt he was dis-appointing his father. All his life Abdel Latif had venerated the great philosophers who had changed humanity, but for his own children he wanted professions that would safeguard them against going without. But Bolbol felt incapable of doing anything differ-ently. He wanted to understand the world, and tried to be one of the best students, but everything went against him: his teachers de-spised thought and sold grades and exam answers to the highest bidders; everything that ran most counter to the essence of philos-ophy existed in abundance in the philosophy department. They despised debate, politics, reflection, and research; the faculty guided students to storefronts where hucksters sold extracts from lectures and where the professors took a commission from every sale. As for the lecturers who tried to reimpose the kind of philosophy that ac-tually provoked reflection, they were either dismissed or finally shut themselves up at home in despair. Student informers wrote reports accusing them of sedition, inciting atheism, and cursing the party as well as Arab nationalism. Thought was a veritable crime, and it necessitated interrogation.

Bolbol soon lost his enthusiasm. He bought lecture notes and followed the teachings of professors who vaunted the ideas and wisdom of the Leader. He didn't dare admit his cowardice to Lamia. When he was with her, he was possessed by his old image of himself, of which nothing now remained but the remnants of his old, dead ambition. He became one of the herd that only wants a degree to get a job. Soon he was employed at the Institute of Food Storage and Refrigeration, where he recorded the quantities of tomatoes and onions prepared for warehousing and then, at the end of the season, would record how many tons had gone bad. It was trivial work that required no philosophy. Bolbol stopped caring about new ideas, and day by day he became a model employee—scared of everything. What frightened him most were those perilous situations in which he found himself agreeing with Lamia when she spoke of necessary change; she would declare loudly that the populace had reached the last stages of servility and that revolution was the only way of uprooting society's backwardness, as well as the dictatorship, and bringing to account the murderers who had plundered the country from east to west. Abdel Latif agreed with her enthusiastically, and Bolbol chorused his agreement, too, but deep down his heart was cold like a rotten quince. How it pained him now, the hypocrisy he had shown on so many positions just to satisfy Lamia and retain the privilege of her friendship. If it pleased her, it was enough for him. Even today, the look she had given him that morning as she bid him goodbye was all he'd needed to hoist his father's body onto his back and carry it through checkpoints, storms, and the arid wilderness.

They were alone on the road again. All other cars disappeared, night fell, and the scene went back to being terrifying. Bolbol felt bleak, Fatima's face plainly showed her apprehension, and Hussein was worried they were lost. They listened to the storm, and none of them cared about the state of their father's corpse or whether it fell off the seat. Blueness now suffused the chest almost up to the neck, but they didn't look at it anymore, so as to avoid seeing the bloating. Hussein had even stopped making proclamations about what time they would arrive. They had traveled more than a hundred kilometers and began to convince themselves they were over halfway there. At this point, they told themselves, mired in the unknown, going on was surely preferable to heading back.

The searchlights of the next checkpoint appeared in the distance. They slowed down. When they reached it, the soldiers on guard looked at the family in astonishment. These soldiers' outfits were different, nothing like the uniforms at the other checkpoints. These soldiers were also poorer looking than they should have been, as if they had been cut off in this part of the world—they were certainly soldiers, as opposed to Mukhabarat or private militia, but they had been stationed here on the front lines in the full expectation they would die. A soldier of no more than twenty opened the car door and examined the body, aghast. He looked at everyone's identity cards, smiled, and said he was from a village near Anabiya; he knew the family name. They exhaled in relief and smiled back at him. He took pity on the dead man and, leaning his head into the car, he told the siblings that at the next checkpoint, which belonged to the Free Army, they should find his cousin Hamada. He might help them secure accommodation till morning; they certainly couldn't keep traveling tonight. Then he raised his hand in farewell and allowed them to pass.

It was fewer than five kilometers to the Free Army's checkpoint. They asked for Hamada and added the name of his village; Hamada came out, looking surprised, and scrutinized the siblings. They introduced themselves and explained their task to him. He asked them if they knew what it meant to be traveling this road at this time of night. He genuinely wanted to be useful to them and offered to help them find somewhere to stay overnight in a nearby village, at least until dawn, when they could proceed with their journey. The siblings were adamant that they had to reach Anabiya before then; the state of the corpse would brook no delay: they had to bury it as quickly as possible if it wasn't to disintegrate entirely. Hamada saw from their faces that they were hungry, so he suggested that they join him for dinner. Hussein asked if Hamada would provide them with a written directive to the following checkpoints certifying that he knew them and requesting facilitation of their passage. Hamada laughed and informed them that his influence extended about five meters from the point where they were parked. Every squadron at every checkpoint had its own system, and such a letter would be disastrous if it fell into the hands of hostiles. At that moment, the siblings realized they were truly in unfamiliar territory.

Hussein agreed to drink some tea and wait a little. After all, it would be no use arriving in the middle of the night; they couldn't very well wake their uncles and cousins and ask them to bury a dead man at midnight. Fatima asked Hamada for some spirits so she could rub down the distended corpse. They drank hot tea, and Hamada supplied them with a small bottle of spirits and some cans of food. He guessed correctly that they were embarrassed to ask anything of people whose appearance so clearly demonstrated their poverty.

Hamada's face was delicate and gaunt. He told them he had defected from the army a year and a half previously and joined this battalion, which had no funding. He said that his cousin at the previous checkpoint hadn't wanted to defect, preferring to stay with the regime—and now, even if he wanted to defect, it would be difficult for him to do so, as snipers lay in wait on every road. Hamada finished by saying that his cousin hadn't visited his family in three years. He said that the two checkpoints were waging a pitched battle for supremacy that was entirely imaginary; they wanted to keep the peace here, but they had been forgotten by everyone else. He would have talked till morning, repeating that the war was a futile bit of madness with no end in sight; it had been a long time since he had seen anyone from his region who would understand how lonely he was. He asked them to look up his father, a good friend of their uncle, when they passed by his village, so they could tell him that Hamada was doing all right. Hamada added that he spoke to his father on the telephone, but a personally delivered message still meant something in that region.

When Hamada bid them goodbye, he warned them to watch out for extremist squadrons, insisting that Fatima cover her hair thoroughly. Hussein embraced him like a brother and wished him victory. The family only realized their mistake after they left the checkpoint, all three siblings thinking the same thing, but afraid to speak the words out loud: Why hadn't they asked Hamada's help in burying the body in the graveyard of *his* village? After the war was over, they could go back to collect the remains. But the ease of their last couple of crossings had given them confidence they had passed the worst. At last, they had reached the liberated areas, and their identity cards were no longer a problem; no one would look at them with contempt and suspicion for being born in S and having roots in Anabiya. Bolbol remembered his father's rousing words: "The children of the revolution are everywhere." They discussed Hamada and his cousin with amazement and sympathy in order to expel any negative feelings that might slip back into their souls thanks to the continuing stormy weather. They weren't alone on the road anymore, or not so completely; at one point they were overtaken by a few modern SUVs scurrying along with fighters inside. One of these pulled alongside, and its occupants waved to Hussein to turn off his lights; they didn't respond to his plea in return to be allowed to travel behind them, and after a hundred meters the vehicle turned onto a muddy side road. Without lights, then, the minibus seemed like a big coffin shared by Bolbol, Hussein, Fatima, and the body. The calmest of the four was the corpse, of course, which knew no fear or worry; blue tinged, it swelled with perfect equanimity and didn't care that it might explode at any moment. When it vanished, at last, it would do so willingly, unconcerned with wars, soldiers, or checkpoints.

Bolbol thought about his mother. She hadn't expected his father's body to be buried beside her. She hadn't even left enough space beside her grave for it.

She had often endured his unjustified rage. The image of them tending flowers in the garden in total harmony was a lie his mother had been forced to live for all forty years of their married life. When she was angry, she would mourn her lot in curt phrases. It took years of Bolbol's hearing these tiny complaints before he came to understand the tragedy of her life: she was a maid to a man who had left his land and his family to invent an imaginary history for himself. She missed Anabiya and its meadows. She didn't care about anything her husband did; she didn't want to become a sophisticated woman. She adored the strong consonants of her country accent and kept silent whenever her husband started to tell his family history to visitors. Believing that he was being creative, not that he was simply a liar, she no longer bothered to correct him as to names and relationships. The only really interesting character Abdel Latif had known was his sister Layla, who had set herself on fire—but he never once mentioned her. She had been a close friend of Bolbol's mother, who described her as a wonderful girl and recalled her kind heart and beautiful voice when she sang for her friends as they prepared okra, squash, and tomatoes on mild summer evenings. Layla had memorized every song, it seemed, and her zest for life made her popular among all the girls her age; they would gather at her father's house, and she would teach them beauty regimens. She experienced an early heartbreak when she fell in love with her cousin, Lieutenant Colonel Jamil, who left her and married an idiotic fair-skinned girl from a powerful family rich in land. Bolbol's aunt told her friends her beloved had essentially sold her, had given her up in exchange for an enormous dowry and powerful connections, but on the day he was executed, she tore her clothes and lamented as a wife would grieve her husband. She couldn't endure the weight of her few memories of Jamil. She stepped up to the coffin, pushed aside the soldiers who surrounded it, wouldn't let anyone near the traitor, and beat on the coffin lid, wanting to wake him as she used to do whenever she could steal a few moments to go to his room. She would shake him awake and stroke his face with her delicate hand, staring at him in a way he found irresistible. Her laughing eyes, her fresh scent, and her strange elegance among the *fellahin* made her seem like someone from a different era and place. She wasn't shabby and second-rate, like the other women of the area.

Her open mourning for Lieutenant Colonel Jamil was a real scandal for the family. She had gone further than a girl of any respectable family was permitted to go. The men gawked at her, her father couldn't hide his fury, and the women of the family took her home, locked her in her room, and returned to the funeral as if nothing had happened. Everyone waited for a verdict from her father and three brothers. All that happened, however, was that her father was silent for a month, then everything went back to normal. After all, Lieutenant Colonel Jamil *deserved* to have girls rending their garments in frenzied mourning on his account (or so the family, which had tasted power for the first time through his advantageous marriage, decided to believe). Six months after this incident, Layla's father informed her that an appointment had been made to recite the Fatiha over Hamdan, after which she would have to marry him in a month's time; she was to accompany the women of the family to Aleppo for the preparations in the meantime. Layla couldn't accept this; she went to her father's room and told him outright she would never marry Hamdan. Then she asked to speak with her brother Abdel Latif and told him that he had to intervene, adding that she wouldn't be turned into a cow in the house of a man she didn't love, and she wouldn't live as her mother had lived. She didn't know what form she wanted her life to take, but she was certain about what life she *didn't* want. She knew her wishes were exceptional but was confident that her brother Abdel Latif wouldn't throw her to the wolves of their family. They spoke for a long time, but he was afraid of being seen protecting and supporting her, which would have been a pointless battle in any case, especially after the scandal of her behavior at Lieutenant Colonel Jamil's funeral. What Layla wanted was to distance herself from this land of ruin and finish her education; she was the only girl in the village who had even gotten through middle school—with the encouragement of her brother, who was now lying dead in a cold minibus on a distant road. Yes, she'd wanted a different life, the one she thought that she deserved. No one believed the threats she made; no one believed that she would really make them regret their decision. She told Bolbol's mother she would become a blazing torch, burning her family and lighting the way for other women.

She used to love long words, just like Abdel Latif. She composed unusual sentences and could spend hours reciting poetry and criticizing the refinement of its composition. She was an inexhaustible mass of sensations. No one could believe their eyes when they saw her on her wedding night. She contented herself with being among her friends, including Bolbol's mother, in the weeks leading up to the wedding; she wouldn't allow any women from the groom's family, or even her own, to help her. She celebrated her body: removed her body hair like the girls in the city did, and Bolbol's mother rubbed her with creams. Then she put on her white dress, went up to the roof, and pulled up the stepladder behind her. She had prepared everything the day before: the bottle of kerosene and the matches. She looked down at the revelers in the courtyard, where the party was at its height, before she began to laugh, and set herself alight. Her body was extinguished amid the stupefaction of the men and the weeping of the women, who couldn't believe they had lost their dear friend forever.

But nothing changed after Layla's suicide. Girls were still made to abandon their education after primary school, their families decided whom they would marry, and any girl who left the herd was slaughtered—but Bolbol's grandfather was no longer the same man. He shut himself away and died ten years later, full of regret that he hadn't taken her threats seriously. He had loved Layla and thought of her as the true heir of his own mother, who used to recite poetry to her husband. Many people still quoted her poetry and sang those sweet songs of hers. As well as composing love songs, she'd sung about many local events, recording them for posterity: the anonymous Storyteller of Anabiya. But no one had corrected the official history, in which her poetry and songs were usually attributed to Bolbol's great-uncle. There was nothing in the history of the region about how that skinny little woman had passed all her anxiety on to her granddaughter decades later, and as for Layla herself, no one said anything about her, save that she had set herself on fire to hide her disgrace.

Now almost everyone was dead. Only a single uncle and a few cousins were left; most had fled for the camps in Turkey or were in prison or had joined the Free Army and its battalions, fighting one another as well as the regime. No one was waiting for the three siblings in Anabiya except for a few men who were already exhausted from burying so many dead over the last four years. But those few men would be enough to witness the accomplishment of Abdel Latif's last request, although they had forgotten him long ago. His occasional family visits to Anabiya hadn't been enough to reestablish the connections he'd broken after Layla's death.

On those visits, Abdel Latif would exaggeratedly praise his new town and its inhabitants, trying to sound as though he'd found a new place to belong. He took no pleasure in fighting, in angry shouting matches. In reality, of course, Damascus did nothing to help him find a new identity for himself, and he ended up living in a small town on its margins, afraid of everything, like everyone who'd fled the countryside. Whenever he ran up against any bureaucracy, he would be asked about his relationship to the traitor Lieutenant Colonel Jamil; he would be struck dumb and reflect how, like him, they must be rather afraid if after all these years they still hadn't forgotten Jamil. In this country, people like to say "The page doesn't turn after death"; the dead pass on their actions and attributes to their children and through them to their grandchildren. Everything you do is closely observed, and your official records may as well be locked behind an iron wall: impossible for any civilian to read or alter.

And in one of the calmer moments of that stormy night in the minibus, it occurred to Bolbol that, as for all citizens, his father's full record would still be in the hands of the Mukhabarat. Bolbol was assailed by a peculiar curiosity. He wished he could obtain those pages and read over them: what they said about Abdel Latif, how it had been more than forty years since he first arrived in S, that small town near Damascus, and then what they had written on the final pages. Thinking about these things distracted him from telling his brother and sister about Nevine, which he'd been meaning to do. It also prevented him from replying to Hussein, who had again worked himself into a rage over their stupidity for not getting rid of the body long before now.

Fatima spoke up to inform her brothers that the corpse was splitting apart. Bolbol immediately tried to change the subject, as if what she had said was of no concern. He wasn't in the least bit interested in dwelling on the state of the body. He'd always known that keeping it intact and in the same state as when they left the hospital two days earlier was simply impossible. And when Fatima took it upon herself—out of her sense of duty, Bolbol supposed— to lift the blanket off of the corpse and reveal the nightmare underneath, which the brothers could only have guessed at, Bolbol wished she would just drop dead as well. The dead turn to shit. And even if Abdel Latif's corpse had *literally* turned to shit, they still wouldn't be able to just wipe him away. Their memories were like acid inside them, boring eternally down into their depths and covering their hearts with pockmarks—just as the sight of Layla burning like a corncob ate at Abdel Latif's heart until the day he died.

Fatima wouldn't leave well enough alone. She kept drawing her brothers' attention to the ragged body, from which a string of pus had started to trickle from a tear. Hussein stopped the minibus, turned to Fatima, and shouted angrily, "Let it! Let it turn to shit!" He cursed his father and his family and glared furiously at Bolbol, who wouldn't meet his eye. Bolbol was afraid he wouldn't be able to bear what Hussein would say next. For some time now, he'd been glowering at Bolbol in the rearview mirror; they hadn't expected to pass another night on the move. Silent tears were, as usual, dripping down Fatima's cheeks, and a peculiar compulsion made Bolbol now decide that he wouldn't go on allowing Hussein to behave however he liked toward them. Bolbol would carry out his father's wish even if he had to carry him to Anabiya himself. He felt greatly comforted by this decision, but he kept silent and wouldn't respond to Hussein's provocation.

Images of their childhood had besieged them ever since leaving Damascus, of course, but now they were positively suffocating Bolbol. They weren't all bad, but with the passage of time, those innocent moments had been made strange. Neither he nor Hussein could save the other; they were two sides of the same coin: Hussein was the face of bravery and buffoonery, and Bolbol of cowardice and capitulation. Both had lost the battle with life. Now all three siblings were like strangers to this corpse that, however much it had lost, still retained the advantage of being able to lie there without caring.

The drumming of the pouring rain was hammering their nerves. Twenty kilometers later the optimism they had felt at leaving the previous checkpoint finally ran out. They were back in the unknown. A group of cars overtook them, speeding erratically along the road. The armed men within had harsh faces and long beards. Their dark complexions made them look like foreigners; only one was fair, with braided hair and a half-witted expression. The siblings slowed down as they neared the cars, looked at the men curiously, and then went on their way. Hussein didn't bother to hide the fact that they were utterly lost. A few lights appeared in the distance, and Hussein said they needed to stop and spend the night in the nearest village. Their nerves couldn't take any more.

They approached a weak light. A man similar to the men they had seen in the cars waved his flashlight at them to stop, and Hussein rolled down his window. The armed man beckoned at him to slowly approach what appeared to be yet another checkpoint. His accent was peculiar, certainly not Syrian. Hussein told his siblings that the man must be Chechen and added that he knew the type from having escorted so many Russian dancers. They reached the checkpoint and waited. Their hearts were thudding almost out of their chests, and Bolbol felt he could almost hear them. A sniper could easily pick them off here. The wait was enough to liquefy anyone's backbone. Who knew what they'd landed themselves in this time. After more than half an hour another vehicle straying through the night stopped behind them. They felt safer when they saw that the three young men inside were civilians like themselves. Hussein wanted to ask them where they were going; talking to strangers would be a good way to make them all feel calmer. Hussein lit his third cigarette and opened the door of the minibus and immediately a disembodied voice ordered him to get back in the vehicle. A few minutes later they were approached by a man wearing black clothes and a mask. He asked for their identity cards in faltering Arabic and caught sight of the body before they'd managed to describe the purpose of their journey. Hussein launched into a lengthy explanation at once. The man spoke into his handheld radio, then pulled the blanket off the corpse. The body had changed again, was covered with lacerations and was oozing pus all over. Its stench billowed out and clogged every nose. Three armed men headed over, got in, and ordered Hussein to drive to the prince's villa at the edge of a nearby village, in the middle of a field, heavily guarded by more masked men. There, they all disembarked and went into the building.

The smell of incense wafted through the entrance hall where they stood, waiting for permission to meet with the prince. The masked guards didn't say a word, as if they were made of wood. Fatima asked them to show her where the bathroom was, and neither their faces nor their fingers, still resting on the triggers of their rifles, moved. Hussein tried to show off his military knowledge and said they were Dushka machine guns, but one glance from a guard was enough to shut him up. They heard a murmur behind a huge door. The only cheering thing about their situation was that the room was very well heated. Luxury was evident in every detail of the villa. Soon the murmurs got closer and a group of Bedouin men emerged from behind the door, thanking the prince and wishing him long life.

After a few more minutes a tall man opened the door for them. It was a kingdom of masks, no faces at all, no details, and no features. Fatima was the most afraid; she hastily adjusted her head covering so it concealed half her face as well as her hair. In her shabby clothes she looked like a poor woman. Exhaustion from the journey showed clearly on the siblings' faces, as if they had traveled five thousand kilometers rather than two hundred and fifty, a journey that ought to have taken two and a half hours at most.

Bolbol was astonished to see Fatima kneel down to greet the prince in imitation of the actresses in historical dramas. The prince, who was also masked and wearing an embroidered robe in a sort of Abbasid style, asked them their business. His tone betrayed his irritation, and from his ponderous accent they guessed he was Afghan or Chechen. One of the guards entered, gave them back their identity cards, whispered something in the commander's ear, and left. Nonchalantly, and in a stately formal Arabic that almost made Bolbol burst out laughing, Hussein stated briefly that they needed permission to proceed so they could get on with burying their father's body before it rotted away entirely. Hussein had been surprised at the prince's question; surely he must know the rules governing burial of the dead according to Sharia? Hussein looked at Bolbol for help, but Bolbol had nothing to say, only telling himself that the insults would never end; the children of the revolution weren't everywhere as his father had said. Here the three of them were, in a strange land, surrounded by foreigners, and they had no idea why they weren't being allowed to bury their father's body.

Hussein went on to mouth a few courtesies, resorting now to the sayings in his beloved almanacs. He spoke about honoring the dead through their burial, but all were astonished when the prince told the siblings, quietly but angrily, that it was suitable for a Muslim to be buried anywhere within the nation-spanning land of Islam, and last wishes like Abdel Latif's were tantamount to heretical innovation. Hussein heartily agreed with him; Bolbol knew Hussein's most fervent wish was to be rid of the corpse at any price. The prince went on to enumerate all the Companions of the Prophet who had been buried away from their homelands. Bolbol tried to speak, but the prince gestured to him to be quiet. Then he sprang a question on Hussein about the number of *rak'at* performed in the prayer for the dead; he asked them about their sect, and they explained that they were from Anabiya . . . then something unexpected occurred. Dozens of missiles thundered nearby. The prince rose and left quickly, leaving the family in his large hall. They wasted no time and hurried out behind him. Hussein waved at Bolbol to go back to the minibus with Fatima. An odd current was running through the people in the building. Hussein told the guards that the prince had given the family permission to leave; they raised no objection, indeed didn't seem to care one way or the other. The bombs were still falling nearby; one of them must even have hit near the villa, for they felt it quaking. The battle was right on the other side of the road but seemed just as likely to intensify and move even closer. The siblings quickly climbed into Hussein's minibus. In their hurry they barely noticed that the vehicle had been thoroughly searched, papers and CDs flung everywhere. They simply made sure their identity cards were safely with them and then sped off without turning on the headlights.

Yet Hussein slowed down again after only a few kilometers. He told the others he had lost the road. Raqqa was nearby, but he wasn't sure which junction would take them to Aleppo. The prince's villa and his village had disappeared from view, but they could still hear shooting and explosions. Hussein felt they should stop for the few hours left until dawn. They needed some sort of guide if they were going to find the road, and anyway—as they were all well aware—traveling with a corpse in the car at this time of night would just arouse more suspicion. He chose a spot near to a number of crossroads and turned off the engine, and silence reigned once more, broken only by the barking of a nearby dog.

It was midnight. Hussein lay down in his seat and closed his eyes. Fatima tried to cover her face. No one wanted to look at the corpse. It had become a plague upon them, nothing less. Bolbol could no longer object if Hussein suggested burying it here, by the side of this unknown road. He heard Hussein snoring for a short while and had no choice but to look out at the night. He tried to get some fresh air and opened the door to step outside, but the intense cold bit into his limbs, and he stayed inside the bus. Their heavy heads were the natural result of the stench that blew over them. They were breathing in death as no one had ever breathed in the death of a loved one; it permeated their skins and coursed through their blood, and Bolbol wondered idly if all three of them had gone completely moldy by now. This was all that remained of his father: decay and pus. Abdel Latif was done with dreams, and these thunderstorms were bidding him farewell on his final journey—a fitting tribute to a misguided warrior. Till his last moment, he had remained proud of all his defeats. He hadn't known a single moment of victory, but he had been intoxicated by it all the same, expecting it to come as inevitably as the fate that brought him to where he was now.

The three of them were unspeakably weary. None of them could bear to even look at the others. Fatima was lying on the floor, her face as blank and wide-eyed as a seal's. She was trying to piece together the fragments of their childhood that kept surfacing within her memory, but Hussein's voice interrupted her scattered thoughts. He asked Bolbol, "And afterward?"

It was true; Bolbol had no idea as to what would happen afterward and told Hussein as much. The drumming rain increased their desolation. Hussein said they had to put the body in the back of the bus. He couldn't quite manage to admit that the smell was making him dizzy. They prodded Fatima, who closed her eyes again after her few words were ignored. They arranged a space on the back seat, and when they began to move the body, they were astonished at how heavy it was, and how many more splits had appeared in its skin, all leaking yellow pus. They opened the door for a few seconds and immediately saw a pack of wild dogs rushing toward them. Howls filled the area, and they slammed the door to escape this almost unreal ferocity. The dogs leaped at the bus, attacking it from all sides. They bared their fangs, utterly enraged, and Bolbol had the feeling they would never leave them in peace again. He suggested to Hussein that they drive away and find somewhere safe and inhabited to take shelter. Hussein didn't reply. He was staring in fascination at the dog currently trying to scratch the windshield. Hussein laughed and began to tease the dog, which only became more furious. Bolbol was disgusted and frustrated. He knew that if the dogs reached the corpse they would tear it to pieces, and he began to feel genuine terror for his father, now reduced to little more than some carrion to be lusted after by wild animals. This was surely the utmost level of decay. After half an hour the dogs had only become more frantic, new ones had arrived, and now a whole pack was laying siege to the minibus.

Hussein began to take the matter seriously when three dogs began to hurl themselves at the windshield in frenzied concert. He started the engine, but the dogs didn't budge. The bus pulled away, and Fatima tried to cover the rear window to block their view, until Bolbol told her that it was the smell that had attracted the dogs when he'd opened the door. How and where would they flee? They chose a road that Hussein guessed would lead them back to the main route to Aleppo, leaving the junction for Raqqa behind them. Bolbol asked, "Why don't we go to Raqqa, and from there to Turkey? We could cross back over at Bab al-Salamah, near to Anabiya?" Hussein sneered at this bright idea, asking how they were going to get a body across the border without a passport.

The dogs were still chasing them. They were driving along a narrow road without any signposts, feeling well beyond lost. Hussein grumbled when Bolbol kept offering suggestions—for example, that they admit defeat for the time being and head back to the junction where they had stopped for the night, arguing that eventually the dogs would get bored and leave them alone. Bolbol saw Hussein scowling in the rearview mirror. It was far too late for them to be having any more adventures; a mistake at this point might cost them their lives.

It was still raining. They reached a junction with an old track that led through deserted fields to a distant village, drowning in darkness. Yes, they had no idea where they were. The dogs had fallen behind, but their distant barking wasn't exactly reassuring. The siblings were more than apprehensive. They were lost in the wilderness.

Hussein resolved to act on his own initiative, deaf to all entreaties. Fatima begged him to eat a morsel of the bread they still had, and he didn't reply. He sank down in his seat and stared at the rain, subsiding at times and intensifying at others. It would take perhaps ten minutes to reach the village, and being somewhere inhabited was preferable to staying in this wasteland. The dogs would inevitably come back; they knew their way to the prey, and unlike the siblings, they had noses that kept them from getting lost.

Bolbol recalled aloud how, in recent months, stray dogs had migrated from the towns surrounding Damascus to skulk in the city. They were not much like dogs anymore; their eyes were wolf-like, and their jaws hung slack. Exhausted and not content with bones, they gnawed at the corpses that were too numerous for anyone to bury, especially after the larger battles. These dogs were no rumor but an established fact, confirmed by many. On the few occasions when he had gone out at night on some errand or other, Bolbol himself had seen them eating human flesh and wandering around the streets with a total lack of concern. Meeting a dog at night was horrifying now; it could be the end of you. When a dog's ferocity and hunger cause it to lose its gentleness, it will never again be content with merely barking. These dogs had tasted human flesh, and they couldn't forget it.

Hussein wasn't listening. He turned off the engine and began to smoke, reflecting on their ongoing disaster. These small unknown roads would get them even more lost. He was completely turned around. Suddenly, he told Bolbol that he was the one who had involved them all in this mess, and he had to take responsibility for it. If they didn't reach Anabiya by the afternoon, he would leave his siblings and the body by the roadside. He added that his father didn't deserve all this attention anyway; he had turned Hussein out of the house and never cared about him again. His voice was level and calm as he glared at Bolbol in the mirror. Bolbol surprised him by saying, "Why not just leave us now."

Hussein turned to his brother and then opened the side door of the bus and tried to drag the corpse outside on his own. While he worked, he made sure to say some horrible things to Fatima, who could still do nothing but cry. This labyrinth wasn't the place to settle scores, but Hussein was determined to throw the body out into the open air. Bolbol got out and was drenched by the rain within minutes, but he retained his self-possession. A strange force had sprouted in his heart, and he felt capable of murder. Yes, for the first time, he felt as though murder might, after all, be the best way to rid oneself of old grudges. He even caught himself thinking that either he or his brother would have to die: that neither Hussein nor he would ever feel safe so long as the other was alive.

Hussein's rage gave him strength. He held out against Fatima's pleading—she had thrown herself back on the bus's floor to kiss the feet of both brothers and was begging them to calm down. She spoke about the family, their father, their relationship, and their poverty, appealing to their noble-mindedness before she choked up entirely. Hussein cursed her and called her a whore, kicked her, and drove her out of the bus, where she fell to the ground. The sight of her, floundering in the mud, crying and unable to get up, was too much for Bolbol. He rushed at Hussein, grabbed him by the collar, and hauled him into the rain. The body, which Hussein had been trying to push and pull outside, fell over again, and their father's face got stuck in the narrow space between seats. Bolbol pushed Hussein onto the ground and kicked him, hard. He was crying now, too, and couldn't stop. Hussein got up and attacked Bolbol like a wild animal. He was solidly built and still fairly well muscled. The brothers struggled and fought for a few minutes before Hussein pinned Bolbol to the ground and punched him enough times to make Bolbol surrender. He let himself lie limp on the muddy ground, watching the overcast sky. He reflected that if his brother did manage to disappear, Hussein could at last distance himself from his childhood and invent the one he'd always wanted. And if Bolbol made it abroad and began a new life, he would be rid of his burdens forever.

The rain and the mud caused his body to lose all sensation. He licked the blood streaming down his face. He heard Hussein sobbing. Now all three siblings were crying. Bolbol wanted to get up but couldn't. With Fatima's help, he managed it after a few more tries. She led him back to the minibus, and Hussein followed them in silence. He started the engine and headed for the nearby village, still in total darkness.

The rain stopped, and the sky began to clear. When they reached the village, they realized it had been abandoned after some catastrophe. The houses were completely destroyed, obviously from aerial bombardment. The remains of furniture were strewn over the muddy roads. Everything was rubble. They proceeded slowly, seeking out anyone who might help them. The village had been small in any case, no more than forty houses lining a narrow paved road with a few other streets leading to a small square. Hussein stopped in this square and left the engine running. He honked the horn a few times in case anyone might still be around, but there was nothing here but desolation. Fatima mopped at Bolbol's wounds with her sweater, still crying silently. Hussein got out to explore. He didn't want to stay with the others; whatever little had remained between them was gone.

They had thought they would have a long time to talk during the journey. It would have been an appropriate occasion for reminiscence; after all, during his life, their father had only been able to gather his children on just such passing occasions, when a sense of duty, rather than desire, had been sufficient to corral them into the same place. Their father wouldn't hear of the seriousness of the rift between them, which grew daily, but this journey with his body hadn't offered either the time or the opportunity to voice their resentments of things that might have seemed small but, after many years, loomed large. Indeed, it had been a surprise to realize that it was four years since they had gathered together on any pretext at all, even for a special occasion. The general climate in the country gave them all an excuse. Families no longer braved checkpoints for gatherings. But the years before the revolution had been no better; none of them knew that they had all secretly wished to leave the family for good.

Bolbol believed, deep down, that Hussein was responsible for the first real crack in the edifice. That infamous night when he had picked up his suitcase and left the house had been a mortal blow to their stability, although later events may have seemed more catastrophic. At the same time, that departure had actually done

Bolbol some good; he felt that it had regained him his position in the house. When Hussein left, the clamor his presence always caused was over; it had been unbearable for a person as sensitive and weak as Bolbol. He had wanted to tell Hussein all the things he had smothered within himself for years, but there hadn't been a point during their journey when it wasn't either inappropriate or simply too dangerous to talk.

For one thing, Bolbol had also been astonished to see that Hussein really couldn't live at home anymore, after that night. And then the lack of anyone's interest or concern about Hussein came as another shock to Bolbol—until he stopped noticing it. Initially he'd believed it was all temporary, and that Hussein would return after a few days. But when Hussein was in prison, it was his friends who had followed up on his case and interceded as guarantors for his release; none of the family cared to do it. And despite all the intervening years, that night had stayed with everyone: never forgotten.

They had spent too long with the body. They were in no shape to continue. When they first set out from Damascus, they had been reasonably optimistic that they would eventually deliver their father's body as promised and were relatively united in their common goal to defend it. But after the first night, holding on to their own selves had become a goal that couldn't be ignored. The corpse was no more than a pretext. Deep down, all three thought that they couldn't sacrifice themselves for anyone. Holding on to their lives, despite the misery of them, was the real goal that everyone harbored.

Hussein walked off, down yet another empty road, and left the square. He came back a little later, climbed into the van, and took them to a house where a gaslight was burning and the door was open. Clearly he had spoken to its owners. He left his siblings in the vehicle and went into the single room left undamaged. An elderly woman came out and beckoned to Bolbol and Fatima to enter. Bolbol considered staying where he was, but Fatima took him by the hand and led him out. She kissed the old woman, thanking her for her generosity in hosting them.

Their father's body stayed alone in the minibus. Bolbol thought that if the dogs managed to find a way in they would tear it to shreds and that he wouldn't lift a finger to defend it; after it was over, he would pretend that he hadn't realized what was happening and that in any case protecting the corpse wasn't his responsibility alone. The others were also Abdel Latif's children and had an equal obligation to guard his remains.

The room was warm. The old woman's husband was inside. The old man and woman had to be about eighty. It was clear that they couldn't hear very well; they couldn't make out everything that the siblings were saying. Fatima behaved like the hostess, making tea and then warming some extra water in the kettle. She bathed her brothers' injuries, which had stopped bleeding. Bolbol saw that Hussein's eye was swollen, and in the large mirror hanging on the wall he saw his own face was full of bruises. They relaxed in the warmth and understood from the old woman that planes had bombed the village a dozen times. Its inhabitants had fled, and only two families remained. They had been waiting to die for many years now.

Gravely, Bolbol asked the old woman if it would be possible to bury their father in her village's graveyard. She was astonished at the question and said that there had been three hundred new graves in the graveyard in the past year alone. The Free Army had entered the village the year before, but hadn't been able to hold on to the territory for more than a year. Three of her grandchildren had fought alongside them, and after the great battle more than a hundred bodies had been strewn over the roads and fields. The villagers who were still alive had buried them before traveling to the camps in Turkey.

When the old woman mentioned the village's name, the siblings realized that they had gone in the wrong direction. The old couple was delighted they had come, however; it had been a long time since they'd spoken to anyone else. They told the story of death, bombardment, and battle with relish, before falling silent and asking the family about Anabiya. In his unadulterated country accent and using old-fashioned words, the man told stories about the time he went to northern Aleppo. He had bought straw there that day, but couldn't remember the name of the person who had sold it to him; the vendor had been determined to host him, as the hour had gotten very late. Although this had happened sixty years earlier, he spoke about his trip as if it had been yesterday and spent considerable time trying to remember the location of the house in case they knew the name of the person who had sold him the straw. The siblings couldn't bring themselves to care. Hussein stretched out on an ottoman and dozed off; when the old woman covered him with a worn blanket, he curled up like a child. The old woman led Fatima to a small larder to prepare some food for them. Bolbol felt warm and relaxed; there were only two hours until sunrise, and he spent them in a short, fitful sleep while their host went on trying to remember the name of the man who had sold him the straw.

They had to settle the matter. If they buried their father here, everything would be over. Fatima had regained some energy and, taking the kettle full of hot water, tried to clean her father's body. It was impossible to master the lethal smell, and the body's remaining fluids were oozing out of even more cracks in the form of diarrhea-like pus.

For the few hours they had spent in the warm room, Bolbol relaxed. Without preamble, he informed Fatima that their father had married Nevine and was shocked at her indifferent reaction, as if he hadn't said anything at all. She just laughed and carried on drinking tea. Hussein heard what Bolbol said but also made no comment. He reflected that the news given to him by his friend Hassan, who had been able to leave S during the siege, had been true. The marriage hadn't been a whim; it was the perfect story of a late love that had healed the wounds of his father's isolation and loneliness.

One day, Abdel Latif had gone with Lamia to the home of his old friend Najib, which was now the local field hospital. He was surprised to see Nevine with a strip of cloth bound around her head, and she seemed like a trained nurse as she cut and sterilized strips of muslin. She was assisting her first-born son, Haitham, the doctor, who was trying to save the wounded strewn throughout every room in the spacious house. Three other doctors, also from the town, had offered their help. The torpor of the mourners, of everyone, had transformed into inflexible rage.

Every family in the town had flocked to the field hospital after the Mukhabarat prevented the state clinics and hospitals from admitting any of the wounded. Everyone offered what they could: staggering quantities of medicines and muslin cloth were collected from houses and pharmacies, medical equipment was transferred in secret from the clinics, and a makeshift operating room was equipped in the basement after it had been cleared of provisions and the old dresses Nevine had carefully packed away ten years earlier after her husband died in a road accident on his way to Beirut.

Nevine was past sixty, still beautiful; there was a proud look in her eye that had sharpened during her marriage, which had been spent in never-ending battles with her husband's family. Haitham had graduated from medical college a few months before the revolution, and her younger son, Ramy, twenty-two years old, had graduated from business school the year before and gone straight into military service. Nevine couldn't bear the loss of Haitham after he was arrested at an air-force Mukhabarat checkpoint—they were notorious for their excessive cruelty—which had caught him leaving the town. When Nevine heard he had been arrested, she was struck with a terrible foreboding. Haitham hadn't known that treating the wounded was a grave crime in the eyes of the regime. In perfect innocence he acknowledged treating them in his family's house, and a week later a telephone call came for Nevine. A high-ranking Mukhabarat officer asked her to pick up her son's body from the military hospital in Mezzeh and then hung up on her.

No one slept in the small town that night. Police and Mukhabarat officers withdrew from the town, and the young people were ready to burn down any building belonging to the regime: the police station, the council building, the houses of informers who were individually known to them, supporters of the party. More than twenty thousand men, women, and children protested and raised their fists in the air in rage while they waited at the town gates for the bodies of Haitham and three of his friends, all murdered under torture in a Mukhabarat facility. One member from each family went to sign a receipt for the body of its son, who had officially died in a car accident or as a result of some mysterious illness.

The large car carrying the four bodies glided along in the

distance. Nevine was sitting in the front seat looking ahead at some invisible point, her face grim and unreadable. Abdel Latif was standing in the middle of the crowd, watching her. His tears streamed silently as his eyes, along with everyone else's, fixed on the bodies that the young men carried on their shoulders through every street, amid angry cries calling for the fall of the regime.

Nevine asked everyone carrying the bodies of Haitham and his friends to bring them to her house. They carried the three bodies and a black bag in which the dismembered lumps of her son's flesh were gathered. She coolly asked Haitham's doctor friends to reassemble his corpse. They tried to convince her that it would be useless. Why would a corpse care about that? Many people had buried whatever remained of their children when they hadn't received a complete corpse—but she was determined, and no one dared to dispute her. She waited for them by the door. The doctors worked for hours in a terrible state of mind. It wasn't easy to put their friend back together. Haitham's body didn't have any fingers, and the fate of those severed fingers remained a mystery, though his face and most of his other limbs had been returned. He had been shot in the back of the head before being cut up. When they were finished, the body was carried out in a shroud. Nevine lifted the shroud from his face and looked into his eyes for the last time, wanting her hatred to reach its fullest extent.

Abdel Latif's eyes didn't leave Nevine's face for a moment. He kept his distance to screen his anguish and didn't approach the mourners who stayed up with the four corpses all night. They put the bodies on a large wooden platform, surrounded them with flowers of every description, covered them with revolutionary flags, and left their faces uncovered. It was the utmost defiance. After the morning prayer, the bodies were buried in the new graveyard constructed on land Nevine had donated on the western side of her house. She now left that building so the whole house could be devoted to the field hospital and moved to her old small apartment close to Abdel Latif's house. She took very few things with her, just enough for a lonely widow in her sixties.

Over the following days, Abdel Latif spent hours every day managing the graveyard. He traced the outlines of walkways between the graves and left plenty of space to plant trees and flowers. He wanted it to be eternal, not just a simple cemetery. He hadn't expected that within two years it would be crowded by one thousand seven hundred graves. He arranged them in two sections: one for the young fighters, most of whom were no older than thirty-five, and another for the civilians killed by air raids, missile attacks, and every sort of heavy weapon used during the unceasing bombardment. Whole families were killed, including children and women and old people who couldn't get away. This territory of death became his whole life, and he spent most of his time looking after it.

At the time of Haitham's murder, when Abdel Latif was able to speak his few words of condolence, Nevine told him she was no longer afraid. Nothing in this life mattered to her anymore. He asked her to leave all the affairs of the graveyard to him and freed her from it completely. He spent his time arranging the paths, planting flowers everywhere, and distributing them over the graves. The graveyard acquired some narcissi, and every morning Nevine would watch Abdel Latif as he worked tirelessly. She expected him to invite her to join him in caring for the basil and rose seedlings. From the moment she had looked into the void, Abdel Latif also transformed and became like her. He no longer had anything to be frightened of. He was the bravest he had ever been. He would visit her in the evening and leave odd things by the door he said she had liked more than forty years before. He would remind her of moments so long past she couldn't remember if they had truly happened—had she really listened to those songs, smelled those roses? There wasn't much time left for the man granted inexhaustible energy by the revolution. He suffered from a surfeit of projects, discussed every detail pertaining to the town, joined every committee, swept the streets with young volunteers, filled placards with his beautiful calligraphy for the Friday protests.

Soon spontaneous protests were springing up almost daily, and in spring 2012 everyone was preparing to celebrate the revolution's first anniversary. The presence of armed men was nothing unusual by then, mostly defectors from the army, young men from the town, and other volunteers. They organized themselves and set up ambushes for vehicles belonging to the army and the Mukhabarat, who could no longer enter the town at will.

The battles intensified with each day. The angry debate between advocates of peaceful revolution and those of armed revolution was decided in favor of the armed faction, which possessed the force necessary to satiate everyone's hunger for revenge. Everything happened so quickly that Nevine couldn't believe armed fighters were wandering the streets at night in such numbers. The sounds of battle, which never stopped once they began, were all around her, and there was no longer any time for mourning. Whole families fled the town as the specter of death hovered over every house; university students left their studies, tradesmen and day laborers their work, and young men of every age and profession left their former lives, all to join the Free Army.

The city changed. Evenings were no longer safe. The columns of fleeing emigrants filled Nevine's heart with desolation. Her second son, Ramy, wouldn't listen to her pleas to leave the country after he defected from the regime army. At his first opportunity, he fled his barracks with some friends and joined a battalion in Deraa. They let him choose between crossing the border to Jordan, reaching the town of S, or fighting alongside them and sharing their fate. He chose the last option without hesitation, believing that every place was the land of the revolution, not just his home village. He was brave while he lived out his revolutionary dreams with his comrades. He didn't give much thought to what might happen to him; after all, everyone already despaired of their lives. Before joining the Free Army, he had seen everything; he needed no one to explain to him the principles of the regime and its army. He had already witnessed the looting and murder carried out by its penniless soldiers. Their orders were clear: kill indiscriminately, not excluding children, women, and the elderly. The last night before his defection, all his options seemed equally untenable. He wouldn't be a murderer of his own people, even if they shot him in the back of the head for refusing. On that great night when he finally escaped, more than forty soldiers defected all at once, and after they reached the other side, they split up, taking different routes and dispersing throughout the country. Some crossed the border into Jordan; others scattered among the armed battalions of the revolution; still others chose to go into hiding or to return to their families despite the difficulty of reaching them. Ramy fought until his last gasp. He was killed while liberating a military security facility in D, a battle that lasted more than twenty hours. Nevine was unsurprised when she heard the news of his death. She had known he wouldn't be able to live after his older brother's death. Their final conversation, three days before he died, had been upbeat. He told her about the comrades with whom he lived in a barren wasteland. He spoke loudly and boisterously, and she could tell he was frightened. He didn't tell her about the upcoming attack, which would most likely be a large battle, but reassured her and promised her he was trying to leave the country. She had been begging him with all her strength to do this; she didn't want him to die, she had already lost enough people, and she had no one left but him. But deep down she knew that death had him in its grip and wouldn't let him go. She was prepared to hear the news at any moment, and the grand words his comrade used to describe his sacrifice meant nothing to her. He had indeed been brave and had indeed fought fearlessly, but in the end he had died and left her alone. This was what she was thinking as she received condolences from the people of S; they had heard the news from their own contacts in the Free Army, which lamented him as a martyr and a hero.

Desolation gripped the land. As she wandered among the destroyed houses, Nevine reflected that she had nothing left to do in what remained of her life. Deep within, an inner void whistled with a cold breeze. She didn't care about the title "Mother of Martyrs" that was bestowed on women in her position. She sometimes wished her sons had been cowards and fled abroad as soon as possible, but at other moments she felt that everything had needed to happen as it did—that this was just another story of mass delusion. The shame and the silence they had lived through for years were exacting a price, and everyone would pay it, executioners and victims alike. Correcting hypocrisy may be hard, but it was inevitable in the end.

Before, she had loved life enough to want to live twice over, but there wasn't a lot left for her to see. She just wanted to see her sons' murderers cowering and afraid, to exchange her fear with theirs. Afterward she would close her eyes and die.

three

BOLBOL FLYING IN
A CONFINED SPACE

They left the village at dawn. The weak light revealed the extent of the devastation. It seemed as if souls were still moaning under the rubble, shreds of clothing and body parts strewn over the abandoned fields and mixing with the skeletons of their goats and mules. The dogs had scavenged what they could and left the rest for the flies. It was complete and utter ruin. They had heard about scenes like this, but here they were facing them and smelling them for the first time in person, and it was quite a different thing. Bolbol felt he should despise the foolishness of what had occurred between himself and Hussein a few hours previously, but he wasn't ready to comment or apologize, and believed that Hussein felt the same;

the grudges in their life had heaped up like worn-out clothes in a locked wardrobe.

The sky was still overcast and black. They regained the hope that the rotting body might eventually reach Anabiya. The grave, to be completed, needed a body. The shroud would give the body a new form, dignified and white. They guessed that it would take about two hours to travel the remaining distance, and then it would all be over. Their cousins would complete the task and bury their dead.

There had been no network coverage since the day before. Anyway, all their phone batteries had run out. Hussein had forgotten to bring his charger, but he hadn't regretted this when he saw that the towers along the road were all destroyed. They had no hope of calling ahead, and even if there had been a connection, it would have been no use. There was nothing to report. They were carrying the body and they were on their way to Anabiya. It was no longer important to get there at a particular time. They had lost their awe of death, and the body no longer meant anything to them—this morning they could have offered it to that pack of hungry dogs without a second thought.

They crossed a number of checkpoints held by the Free Army without difficulty. The fighters were good-natured and sympathized with their misery. They would uncover Abdel Latif's face and then cover it back up immediately, unable to bear the sight or stench. The siblings' identity cards came in handy here, at last; Anabiya was an influential region, and many of its sons were fighting in the Free Army, based in the countryside north of Aleppo.

When on rare occasions one of the local soldiers insisted on uncovering the entire body, he would see the scars and the splits and the marks on its face—the result of falling from the seat when

Hussein was trying to toss it in the mud—and assume Abdel Latif had been murdered under torture. No one would have believed this was the corpse of a man who had died peacefully in a hospital in the heart of the capital and that it was the neglect of his children and their utter lack of guile that had caused its current degradation.

In any case, carrying a health hazard that needed to be quarantined as soon as possible was a great help in speeding up their journey. Aleppo appeared in the distance, along with pistachio fields, traces of bombardment, and more widespread destruction. The sight of the ruined city revived their sense of connection to the region. They reached Aleppo just before ten. Fewer than seventy kilometers separated them from Anabiya. The closer they got, the stronger they felt; they were not strangers to these fields, their relatives were not far away, and here the family name was tantamount to an identity card in itself. Almost everyone was a relative under the pavilion of their clan, which always strove to uphold its connections—if little else.

Bolbol breathed a sigh of relief, opened his small window, and filled his lungs with the clean air of the countryside. The soldiers at the last checkpoint had urged them to take the outer road, which twisted and turned around the villages before it arrived at Anabiya; entering Aleppo itself would embroil them in another labyrinth they might not easily escape. They didn't know the road, but many travelers along the way helped them keep to it. They tried to hold off the feeling of power that comes from belonging to a herd; the closer they got to Anabiya, the more they tried to return to themselves, and reflected on their estrangement from this place that they didn't really know. And sure enough, Bolbol's eternal fear, that longtime companion, came back to him. He wished his own house were nearby; he would have bathed and purged his body of every stink that clung to him—from the body, the family, the revolution, and the regime—and gone back to his private peace and quiet. Fear might be his final haven, and it might even give him happiness. What had he cared about after he lost Lamia? He asked himself this, and his reply was: Nothing. The regime allowed him to eat and drink whatever he wanted, to spend his free time watching old Egyptian cinema. That little was enough for him; what would be gained by freedom? He had lost all his dreams, and it was difficult to break his cocoon and re-form himself. It was all too late. He was over forty, and all his dreams found expression in his own small house. His father had done a good thing by dying, Bolbol went on to reflect. They would sell his property—even if his big house was rubble now, the land was still worth something—and it would fetch enough for each of them to buy a small apartment in some poor area. Fatima would have to be content with a half-portion, as Sharia decreed; there was no way Hussein would allow her to dispute it. For some time now, Hussein had been dreaming of demolishing that hated house after his father's death. Since his expulsion from it, it held nothing for him but bad memories. He had never gone back.

Bolbol was sure he was overthinking everything, as usual. He told himself he was a spider dangling in a web of forgetfulness. His absence wouldn't cause pain to anyone; no one remembered him apart from Lamia, and even when she asked about him every now and then, it was a form of pity, nothing more. She needed him to prove to herself that she was still needed by others. The neighborhood vendors offered mute responses to his greetings; they might not hate him, but they had no affection for him either. He needed this web in order to be rid of the smell of his wife, the smell of the house they had shared that he hadn't ever wanted to live and die in. Of course he cared nothing about it and fled it very easily. He hadn't ventured any comment on it and spent seven years with his wife in a state of capitulation, raising no objection to the sofas she chose, the pictures she hung on the wall, or the plastic flowers she liberally distributed in every corner—though he found them strangely irritating and daydreamed about throwing them away. Their seven years together had been meaningless. Bolbol could now admit that he had been afraid of her, a peculiar kind of fear; he felt he didn't deserve her, even though she was exactly like most other women.

Within a few months of marrying, they had nothing to talk about other than television serials, which they both followed closely so as not to discover that they had been living in entirely different worlds from day one. They wanted to get the nuisance of living over and done with. His wife dreamed of the moment when she would lie on her deathbed, clasping Bolbol's hand: a rusty, sentimental image, and a common self-indulgence for people who worry that they might end up forgotten, that they're nothing more than an encumbrance to be tossed aside into oblivion. Bolbol's wife was prepared to sacrifice her entire life for this indispensable, dramatic image. She always said, with hope in her voice, "Goodness me, we're aging so quickly!" For her, life had three moments: birth, wedding, and death. What came in between was an isthmus that had to be crossed with a minimum of inconvenience. The only distinguishing characteristic Bolbol had liked about his wife was her lack of demands on his time and thoughts. She was content with not too much sex, considering it a method of communication at best, not a pleasure that should be experienced as fully as possible, at leisure and via all the senses.

The closer they got to Anabiya, the more oddly dejected Bolbol felt. A deep feeling of guilt weighed on him, although he didn't know why. Perhaps because of how he had distanced himself from Abdel Latif in his final years, and for no good reason. His father had suggested that Bolbol come back and live with him in the big house after his divorce, but Bolbol had made do with staying there for a few months before returning to his isolation. He had wanted to discover another self inside himself, the self he'd imagined throughout his life in his daydreams. He imagined himself brave like Zuhayr, worthy of a woman like Lamia, or foolish like Hussein, or a thinker like Sadiq Jalal al-Azm. He had adored the great man's books and way of life, a life Bolbol knew nothing about but still imagined, as he imagined so much else. He spent years alone in total isolation, drinking cheap booze on the weekend, eating cold, stale food, playing with himself, and getting more and more afraid. He couldn't drop down to earth, and he wasn't able to fly, as though he were hanging from a rusty nail in the sky.

Once, Bolbol hadn't enjoyed being alone, but he soon became more involved than he should have been in the search for his definitive form. Simply put, he hadn't done anything; his existence was tantamount to a vacuum. All he had done was observe other people's lives and discover they were like him: a collection of walking lumps taking up space, spending their lives striving to negate death. They repeated the same actions day in, day out, and when, like him, they noticed that time was passing, they made some futile gesture toward extricating themselves from their addiction to daydreaming instead of living—that ultimate human weakness. Faith was the path that came closest to providing some small comfort, but there, too, Bolbol didn't know how to take the first step. It would have taken a powerful faith to stave off the questions that kept him awake at night, not a half faith. He noticed the faces of his neighbors, when they returned from church every day, were more worried than they had been beforehand; even worship hadn't rescued them from their nagging questions, it seemed. It pleased Bolbol to affect a talent for reading human nature, but his lack of conviction in the truth of his intuitions always returned him to square one.

His daydreams became more and more all-encompassing. In them, his body was made anew; it was beautiful, slender, strong. In narrating his fantasies to himself he didn't mind one bit that he was borrowing clichés from the so-called plebs, especially because for the purposes of his daydreaming he had also purloined for his personal use a few of the gorgeous sculpted models appearing on the endless television commercials. Though sometimes, too, he imagined himself transported back to an earlier, more refined era, rather than indulging in the vulgarity of a modern-day setting, and considered himself outstandingly sophisticated for doing so—but manufacturing the past required an energy and imagination he had to admit he didn't possess. It is hard to discover that your self is nothing but a delusion. You consider yourself aloof from the oppression and power of the masses, but in the end you realize any individuality you might have perceived is a lie and that you're just one more worn-out pair of shoes walking the streets. Bolbol felt oddly comforted when his crowded daydreams finally spat out these conclusions shortly after he turned forty-two, and he realized all of a sudden that time had passed and he had never asked himself what he had been doing all these years.

For seven years, Bolbol had lived in the same alley where Lamia had lived as a student. Most of its residents were immigrants, penniless soldiers, public-sector employees, and *fellahin* who had migrated to the city from their distant villages. Most were Christian, but Druze and Muslims of all sects had moved in over the previous thirty years. Although the alley itself was no longer solely Christian, it had retained its churches and Christian graveyards.

When Bolbol went outside, he became a different person. He smiled at everyone walking on the street, didn't raise his voice to the grocers, averted his eyes when a woman passed him, and tried to help small children if he saw them stumble and fall. He thought that creating a good impression would help him to form friendships and forge a sense of belonging in his new neighborhood, but in his daydreams he lusted openly after all the women. He wished he were one of those men who chased every girl who dared to show her thighs to passersby. He would wait for an opportunity to take his neighbor Samar home after she finished work at the Post Institute so he could grope her under the stairs, bare her breasts, and bury his face in them—or, rather, he liked to pretend he might be the sort of reckless libertine who might do just that. But despite his kindness and his increasing flattery, his careful demeanor and his elevated morals, no one ever acknowledged him. They saw him as merely pathetic, another lost soul searching for some peace away from his rural family.

And yet, even still, he didn't know why his heart sank the closer they got to Anabiya. Maybe it was this: he didn't want to see his father's final defeat, returning after more than forty years to a home he had willingly left in search of himself—a self that was admittedly just a collection of slogans borrowed from a past era, but a self that his father had clung to nonetheless. It's hard to admit your emptiness after half a century of delusion, to be reduced to a suppurating mass giving out foul odors, with maggots sliding in and out of your sides . . . Putrefaction is the real insult to the body, not death.

Now Bolbol understood why bodies are shrouded before burial. It is the last moment of dignity, the last image the deceased's loved ones should preserve before the body disappears from their eyes forever.

Bolbol looked at his watch; it was just after ten o'clock in the morning. The first opportunity he'd had in three days to indulge in one of his preferred imaginary scenarios—the ones in which he was handsome, reckless, and successful. Hussein's scowls in the rearview mirror were beside the point. Bolbol felt their task and their relationship would come to an end at the same time, as if their father had arranged it this way, giving them these three days to explore everything between them. And yet, contrary to this, he felt their relationship was the best it had ever been. Their fight had purified their souls of the residue of the past. Bolbol told himself that they had needed one last battle to go back to how they had been, two children who could erase a train from existence with the scribble of a pen or perhaps draw a calf on skis. People accepted all sorts of irrationality from children, as if respect for the imagination was bound to age alone. If they had remained children, neither would be afraid of the other.

Fatima closed her eyes and dozed for a few minutes. She, too, was afraid of reaching Anabiya. In a few hours she would be a true orphan. She couldn't rely on her brothers; they weren't selfish, just enormously weak. In fact, she thought, the presence of a single weak sister would have suited them perfectly, if they were strong. The strong always like to surround themselves with the weak, the better to demonstrate their strength.

Bolbol heard Hussein wake Fatima and ask her to get their identity cards ready; they were nearing a checkpoint. Bolbol opened his eyes and straightened up in his seat. He was happy to ignore

Hussein, who wasn't bothered by this and let him carry on day-dreaming. Things went faster than expected. Hussein was smiling as he took the arm of a soldier, and they walked toward the mini-bus. The fighter was a relative on their mother's side, one of the many defectors from the regime's army in that area. He was a raw recruit, no more than twenty-two, and his strong rural accent reminded them of their father as he greeted them politely and introduced himself. Wisely, he ignored the deplorable corpse. He spoke into a radio to arrange a smooth and quick passage for them and told them about the upcoming checkpoint. He said that extremist fighters harassed travelers and advised the siblings to keep quiet and ignore any provocations. The villages they passed through were deserted. Most houses had been destroyed, and those that were left had been abandoned. They bore the marks of fierce battles. They could smell fresh death and saw clear signs of mass graves. Everyone wanted to forget and make the time pass quickly so this nightmare would be over. They easily passed the next checkpoint. By now they were very close to Anabiya, but they didn't recognize these villages or these roads. Nothing awoke any feeling in them, everything was the same, even the colors of the *fellahin*'s clothes were the same. Bolbol ignored Hussein's anxiety; they were lost, the road was almost empty, and he simply wanted to be rid of his burden and go back to his other life. Bolbol tried to scrutinize Hussein's face. He guessed that it was the last time he would see him. There was nothing between them anymore, but he was exhausted. He, too, wanted to be rid of the body, to be absolved of his promise to his father to bury him with his family, but he still felt moments of awful tenderness for their distant childhood. Images overlapped in a peculiar fashion; memories of his mother escaped him altogether, not wanting to keep still long enough to form a picture of them all as a family. Bolbol told himself that even mental pictures can be torn up: he couldn't get all of them into a single image. They had never been happy, and everything they'd revered was a fantasy. Hussein had rid himself of this delusion, only to exchange it for another. But the fact was that their father hadn't ever been as perfect as the image *he* had cared for more than the truth. He had been cruel; that was all. Burdened with constant fear of his past, present, and future.

In his later years, Abdel Latif had begun to renew his connections with Anabiya. He contacted his cousins, assured himself about his nephews and nieces. Abdel Latif felt a tenderness toward his hometown, but his pride prevented him from allowing himself the happiness of spending his last years near the graves of his loved ones: his wife, his sister Layla, his father, and his older brothers and sisters, of whom the only one still alive was Nayif.

At eighty years old, Nayif was still performing the same function, welcoming the prodigal sons of late family members. He would play this role dozens of times, sitting in the large room of his house, welcoming mourners and pointing out all the rules they would need to comply with, waiting for the relatives who lived far away and informing them of the necessity of undertaking their sacred duty. These were the only moments he could once again be the head of a family, venerated by all. He woke up at five every morning, ate breakfast, and walked to the graveyard to recite the Fatiha for everyone. He completed his promenade with a vain search for someone to talk to. Most of the young people had already abandoned the town for Aleppo. It was futility after futility for him. The days, all alike, accumulated, and he grew cynical while waiting to die. He retold the same stories he had already told thousands of times in the same words. And here he was now, waiting for the body of his last brother, so he could bury it. Abdel Latif would be the least painful, as Nayif's memories of the man didn't extend beyond childhood and youth. And, after the burial, Nayif would, as usual, disappear inside his house for a few months, waiting for his own death to arrive—a death that had already overlooked him so many times before. If he could only learn to forget, it might help him live longer; really, the best route for everyone would be to sweep away the dark rubble of memory and leave nothing behind but the clean white page Bolbol had spent his entire life trying to dream up for himself.

In these dreams, Bolbol once cast himself as part of another family—a family with a single, unified identity. In this family, Lamia was always mistress of his house and mother of his children. He even used to imagine it was Lamia in bed with him when he slept with his wife. But the more he repeated this dream, the more he summoned up her scent, the more it all lost its efficacy. Lamia, with her slim face, delicate lips, and slender body, became more like an affectionate mother than a sexy woman—useless for a man trying to get himself off on a lonely night.

The corpse was unbearable. It had endured three full days. The bloating was so bad now that the body looked as though it might burst at any moment. If it had been in the open air, the smell would have attracted every scavenger for kilometers around. Fatima held her nose, and Hussein opened the window to let out some of the intolerable stench. The body had turned into a putrid mass, no longer appropriate for a dignified farewell. It would be enough to recite a quick prayer over it and to throw a handful of earth into the grave and run.

They passed through more villages and were bewildered at seeing black flags raised over buildings both far away and nearby, along with the skeletons of tanks and burned-out military cars, all remnants of a battle that testified to its ferocity. For many of the dead, these desolate plains had been the last thing they had seen. Bolbol wasn't in a serene-enough mood to think about them. They arrived at the next-to-last checkpoint, where huge cement blocks distributed over the road were forcing the cars down to a crawl. Armed men appeared nearby and in the distance, aiming their rifles, all clothed and masked in black. Their headcloths indicated they belonged to an extremist group occupying much of the countryside to the north and east of Aleppo that was renowned for its terrifying ruthlessness.

The siblings waited their turn in silence. They no longer had anything to say; silence was the token of their desperation and fear. Hussein asked Fatima to cover up completely, and she wrapped her headscarf around her face. A masked man carrying a heavy gun opened the door of the minibus and immediately stepped backward, alarmed at the stink. He asked them to pull over and get out. He spoke with one of his comrades, and then three more armed men approached. Their accents revealed they weren't Syrian. One of them, a Tunisian, tried to speak in formal Arabic. The siblings explained again that they were on their way to Anabiya to bury their father's body, and they proffered their documents and identity cards. The Tunisian asked where in Damascus they lived, and they told him proudly that they lived in S, thinking the name would facilitate an easy passage through the checkpoint. He spoke with someone over the radio. He told Fatima to stay in the van and Hussein and Bolbol to follow him to a nearby building, where he asked them to wait.

Hussein and Bolbol sat down on a bare wooden sofa and proceeded to wait for more than five hours. Masked fighters passed back and forth, and while nothing about them pointed to their specific character or nationality, everything indicated their identity: their black clothes and masks, their long beards. They came and went from a large room in the heart of the building. Time passed with a peculiar slowness. No one spoke to the brothers. The building, which in the past had been some sort of governmental office, had been turned into the local headquarters of the extremist organization in control of the area. Guards emerged from the lower levels accompanied by blindfolded prisoners in chains, exhaustion clearly marked on their bodies and what was visible of their faces.

Hussein and Bolbol were more than ordinarily confused at this latest setback. Hussein tried to speak to one of the soldiers, but the man just glanced at Hussein in bemusement before continuing on his way. Later, this same man came back and beckoned them to follow him. They went into a small room containing a large table and a laptop and a single chair on which a masked man sat in full field uniform, turning over their identity cards. He spoke to them in a laughable attempt at formal Arabic, in an accent not too far away from their own, trying to enunciate each word properly. He said they would submit to being questioned about their religion and added that if they could simply answer a few questions correctly they would be allowed to pass. He didn't add anything else but waved at the masked fighter to take them to the Sharia judge's room for questioning. Before they left, he said that the organization was aware of their father's membership in the Baath Party fifty years earlier; equally, they knew they were also relatives of the late Lieutenant Colonel Jamil, who had been executed by the government forty years before. The past was catching up with them. Hussein now knew that their family name would hardly serve as a password among these people; it might even be a hindrance. They could be detained on account of the delusions of dead family members. He guessed at the identity of the man who'd ordered their transfer to the judge; Hussein was certain it was one of the three men from S who had joined this organization.

They left the room, trailing behind the fighter, who led them to another building. A large sign hanging on the door read SHARIA COURT. A group of women and men were waiting in a corridor, and despite the crowding, silence pervaded everywhere. The brothers moved through the crowd and, behind their escort, turned into a narrow passage that opened onto a large, dusty courtyard off which opened a number of doors, evidently locked. Huge men guarded these doors, their fingers on the triggers of their automatic rifles.

Bolbol entered the courtroom first; their escort asked Hussein to wait. Without preamble, the judge asked Bolbol simple questions about how many *rak'at* should be performed at each prayer time. Bolbol was taken aback. He counted and made a mistake in his answer. The judge asked him outright if he prayed and undertook all his religious duties, and Bolbol replied without fear that he did not, apart from fasting at Ramadan and giving alms. The judge asked him the extent of these alms, and Bolbol wasn't sure what to say. The judge then made him listen to a short recitation of the Qur'an and asked him which verse it was. Silence reigned as the judge waited for an answer. Finally, he asked Bolbol his opinion about this organization. Although Bolbol knew it would take all his courage to get out of this mess, he felt himself slipping into a deep, dark hole. Without a word, he allowed himself to creep slowly into this abyss. Speaking, he knew, would not be to his advantage. The judge directed a few more questions at Bolbol, who had no answer for any of them. He thought of saying something along the lines that, to him, religion meant good conduct, integrity, and devotion, but nothing came out. What he wanted was to slip back into his daydreams.

Bolbol's refusal to speak was irritating the judge. At last the accused summoned up all his energy and tried to explain about the body, about bringing it home to be buried, and Bolbol then affirmed that he would in future take care to carry out all his religious obligations; he would pray at every prayer time, he would listen to recitations of the Qur'an, and he would commit it to memory, as he had done when he was a child. The judge pointed. The fighter who had brought the brothers to court blindfolded Bolbol with a leather strip and took him through one of the rear doors and down a few steps. Bolbol heard a door clang and then felt a hand shoving him inside a cell.

Hussein passed his examination successfully. The judge asked him about how he performed his religious duties, and Hussein replied vehemently that he was a good Muslim and performed all his duties; he correctly explained the number of *rak'at* and the right way to perform ablutions, and thanked God fervently for the blessing of Islam. He was allowed to leave. As he left the court, the judge told Hussein to forget about his brother; he would be staying behind to complete a religious reeducation course.

Hussein left the building. When he reached the van he was astonished to find that Fatima had been struck mute. Five hours of waiting had paralyzed her vocal cords. She could only point to the corpse, from which dense clusters of maggots were slithering. Hussein set the minibus in motion and fled that horrifying place like a fugitive. He was afraid the maggots would soon be chewing on himself and his sister as well. He didn't much mind that Fatima was mute. He assumed it was only temporary, the result of too many shocks. At the next, "last," checkpoint, he asked one of the guards to help him call his family. There was only a short distance left to Anabiya. The maggots were multiplying uncontrollably, it seemed, climbing the windows of the bus and covering the seats. Fatima moved to the front, tried to speak, and couldn't. She knew she would never be as she was. She was mute, and that was that. She lost all desire to try speaking again and surrendered to her new world.

Hussein managed to get through to one of his cousins, who promised to come and meet him at the checkpoint. Hussein now disavowed all personal responsibility for the corpse. He couldn't wait for the dawn. He couldn't spend another night in a place where death was so rife, whose only inhabitants were widows and orphans. He felt every ounce of the idiocy of bringing his father's body all this distance. It was the same old story here: the houses on both sides of the road were utterly destroyed, all the villages were abandoned, the marks of aerial bombardment were clearly visible, and no one cared about the skeletons.

Hussein didn't have to wait at the checkpoint long. Car lights gleamed in the distance, and he felt oddly relieved when his cousin Qasim strode toward him, armed, with three other cousins. Hussein realized that his young cousin had grown up quite a bit in the past four years; he remembered a shy teenager trying to convince his family to let him finish his studies abroad. Now he wore a long beard. The cousins were shocked at the terrifying number of maggots crawling from the corpse and all over Fatima, who had given up and no longer bothered trying to brush off the ones clinging to her clothes. They wasted no time in asking for the details of the difficult journey. Qasim asked Fatima to switch to the other car; Hussein told his cousin that Bolbol had been arrested at the checkpoint of the Islamic extremists. The cousins exchanged glances and decided to handle the matter quietly, assuring Hussein everything would be fine, and there was no need to worry. The remainder of the trip took less than an hour. They didn't stop at the checkpoints along the way but made do with a quick greeting to Qasim's colleagues, also armed, who all exchanged a few words of condolence with him. There was a swift discussion in the other car about Bolbol and some ambiguous words about future interventions and threats should Bolbol continue to be detained. Fatima was afraid for Bolbol. She had surrendered to her own fate, but his rested in the hands of a family he didn't know and who didn't know him. Still, custom decreed that their northern bloodline, blighted since time immemorial, should be defended.

Hussein regained his equanimity. He tried unsuccessfully to forget about Bolbol. He kept thinking of how close they had been back in childhood, though there had also been all their petty fights as a result of Hussein constantly teasing his brother for his puny size, sage opinions, and perpetual good manners. It was in their childhood that they found safety and comfort—more so than in their present and future, anyway; it was the only thing they had, they thought, that others might envy them. But the truth was, that too had been an illusion; theirs had been no different from any other lower-middle-class childhood, with a mother darning their socks and letting out their clothes as they grew, and a father whose delusions dictated his life and made him overlook all sorts of telling details. He was sure that his children would become noted in society, but the time when that might still have been possible was definitively over. The only one left of Abdel Latif's generation was his brother Nayif, who had refused to leave his village. He cared for the graves of his siblings and friends, buried them quietly, and held one *'aza* after another in the living room that hadn't changed since his youth.

The road was easy despite the winter storms and the rain that never stopped falling all night. Hussein relaxed. In the end, the body would be safely delivered to its rightful place after all. At midnight, when they reached Anabiya, the lights were on in Nayif's house. They heard the murmurings of the men who were waiting inside for the body and the sound of cups of tea being passed around. Qasim was strict and prevented anyone from seeing the body. He decided that the burial would take place at the morning prayer; they were used to burying the dead at dawn, as air raids rarely started before seven in the morning. Another young man went with him to the graveyard to dig the grave. Qasim paid no attention to his father Nayif's instructions, nor to his late uncle's wishes. Abdel Latif had chosen to be buried in his sister Layla's grave, or so Hussein had told them, whereas Nayif ordered his son to bury Abdel Latif next to their mother's grave, in accordance with their mother's wishes. She had died forty years before and had mentioned she wanted her children's graves to be near her own. But the armed young man considered such wishes an outrageous luxury. The grave Qasim dug for his uncle was distant from his other family members and easily lost among the profusion of graves. Layla stayed alone, aloof, and repudiated, surrounded by empty space on all sides. Every now and then, unknown young people would plant a rosebush on her grave, but it would soon wither and die. Her tale lived on despite the family's efforts to erase it. Stories here might change over time, might be told in new ways, but they never died. Hussein seemed content and basked in the praise for being so brave in carrying out his father's last wish. Nayif spoke briefly to Hussein and suggested he and Fatima sleep for a few hours; tomorrow would be a hard day. Most of the village's inhabitants had left, but they still had to hold an 'aza and wait for relatives and friends. Before Hussein fell asleep, he heard shots being fired in the air and movement in the next room where they were washing his father's body before shrouding it. He clearly heard his cousins say the maggots should be killed in boiling water. More bodies arrived, fighters from the village who had been killed on distant battlefronts. Hussein heard voices discussing the names of the new casualties, but he didn't care. He curled up like a hedgehog and tried to sleep. His body was exhausted and his soul perturbed, and a terrible estrangement from everything and everyone around him had taken root. He wished he could go right home in the morning. He didn't want to see Bolbol or Fatima ever again; he didn't want to know anything about his father's grave or to visit it and care for it. He slept and no longer heard the loud voices. The volleys of gunfire were repeated, announcing the arrival of more bodies; or maybe they were the same bodies and their comrades were chasing away their fears by putting new holes in the sky, Hussein reflected, without caring either way. He had a strange dream he wouldn't forget for a long while: Bolbol was floating, swimming in the sky and smiling, free as a bird. He was like an angel as he swam in space, scattering roses over the hordes of pedestrians in the Salhiya quarter of Damascus.

But at that very moment, Bolbol was convinced that his death was imminent. He had no hope of leaving this cell, which contained more than twenty prisoners who had committed terrible crimes indeed: One of them had been caught drinking in an olive grove—his breath had given him away at the checkpoint. Another had cursed God in the souk. The rest, like Bolbol, hadn't observed their religious duties, though they seemed less afraid than the other condemned and acted largely indifferent. Most of them had been here for some time, waiting for an end to the negotiations that might secure their freedom. Strangers lost on the road, sons from families who had tried to flee across the Turkish border, others accused of being agents of the regime: they all lined up every morning in the religious classes given by a sheikh who cursed them and called them "deviants from the true path." From his first moment in the cell, Bolbol's senses felt as though they had frozen solid. He couldn't sleep in such bitter cold.

In the early morning, the door was opened, and a huge prison guard ordered the prisoners to get up; it was time for ablutions and the dawn prayer. Everyone performed their ablutions, including Bolbol, who thought the icy water might end him entirely, but he endured the pain in silence and didn't exchange a word with anyone. He was deeply upset, paid no attention to what was happening around him, having surrendered to his fate. He reflected that he wouldn't feel too sad about it if he were killed.

It had been the winter of 2012 when, for the first time, he began to question the worth of what was happening throughout the country. The images of the young murdered protesters were engraved on his memory, and other pictures of crowds of mourners with bullets raining down on their heads. With equivalent hysteria, regime supporters called for even more brutality. On their websites, he read articles written by boys and young men who appeared to come from educated families, judging from their Facebook pictures. They castigated the regime for not having burned Deraa to the ground, adding sardonic recommendations about turning the city into potato fields. The majority of regime supporters approved the idea of burning the country from north to south, applauding the slaughter as if they had tremendous confidence in victory. This hope had been diminished four years later, but they still called for various cities to be pulled down on the heads of their inhabitants. On the opposite side, there were other groups undertaking the same actions, calling for regime supporters to be burned in their beds and cheering their murder. Bolbol would muse on this in silence and wonder what could be achieved by either side through a victory oozing with blood.

Bolbol reflected that when the walls of fear around you crumble, there's only a strange emptiness inside. Nothing can fill it but a new type of fear, perhaps. You don't know what to call it, but it's still fear, no different in flavor, really, than the old type. It makes you feel you're the only one afraid in a tide of humanity that regards dying as the ultimate solution to the enigma of living. And it was true, mass murder or suicide could be a kind of solution, Bolbol supposed. He often imagined whole communities committing suicide in protest against a life so soiled. He himself couldn't bear living among a human flood goaded to such massacres, who evoked old feuds from the depths of history to justify their own slaughtering. He was convinced this was his own personal problem, not the problem of humanity as a whole: each human losing themselves, then finding themselves again by banding together with the other humans who seemed to most resemble themselves, or else transforming themselves in order to resemble those groups . . . all drowning in emptiness.

He had watched his neighbors in the first days of the revolution and heard a large and astonishing collection of slogans it was impossible to believe, broadcast by all as if they were fact. His astonishment was redoubled when he saw men, whose names indicated they were members of the ulema, the religious authorities, appear on state television to analyze and confirm this propaganda to the delight of the heavily adorned female broadcasters who seemed confident of the upcoming victory. Bolbol couldn't bear the commentaries that stated that the protesters had taken to the streets purely under the influence of drugs. One analyst took two hours to explain how the government of an unnamed reactionary country had promised each protester five hundred liras and a kebab to take part in a conspiracy to overthrow the regime. It was easy enough to blindly direct the herd of supporters anywhere you wanted them to go. Questions almost choked Bolbol. For him, the most disturbing thing was the fear that grew and embedded itself in his depths. Several times, he felt a pressing need to speak to Lamia and admit that whenever he went outside, he worried his neighbors would rape him. He avoided even looking toward the windows, and the obsession with spying he had enjoyed for several years no longer interested him. It was fewer than fifty meters from his house to al-Harra Square, where he waited at the stop for the official bus to the institute, and where he returned after work on the same bus to the same spot. On weekends he shut himself away in his house, keeping the windows open so the neighbors could have no grounds for suspecting he was hatching some conspiracy. He was utterly exhausted by defending himself and imagined everyone was watching him, but at the same time he was incapable of moving elsewhere. Renting a house to a man with his identity card would be considered a crime, and he couldn't go back to S. He couldn't bear to look his wretched neighbors' victims in the eye as they were cursed so loudly and openly. Several times Bolbol hid his background, inventing stories about there being a mistake in his paperwork, how he wasn't born anywhere near S . . .

Now here he was, walking with a bowed head alongside twenty others to be taught how to pray at gunpoint. He performed his freezing ablutions, following the instructions of someone in a mask, and felt ridiculous as all the prisoners lined up behind another masked man who explained each step of the prayer. Everything was ridiculous . . . After prayers, what would these people do with them? Would they kill them? Would they exchange them for ransom? Would they make them into slaves? Bolbol didn't care in the slightest; to him, the imperative thing was that by now his father's body would be underground, embracing the bones of his beloved sister, whose burning image had given him sleepless nights till his dying day. Yes, surely not a day had passed without his being reminded of his cowardice. His failure to defend her made him complicit in her suicide, and her choice to burn on the roof on her wedding day was a clear message to everyone: she would never forgive them. She could have committed suicide in a myriad of ways, but she wanted her story to live. She wanted to die in flaming defiance of the lies that would be told about her; she had chosen to die rather than live with a man she didn't love.

Shortly after the sunset prayer, the guard came in and asked Bolbol to follow him. He walked behind the guard unquestioningly and was led to the room of a man who called himself a Sharia judge, where his uncle Nayif was waiting for him, having signed a pledge to instruct his nephew in his religious duties. His uncle kissed him and embraced him, offered his belated condolences, and took him by the hand, and they left. His cousin's car was waiting outside. Everyone called him by his original name, Nabil, which he had almost forgotten, it was used so rarely. He liked regaining his original name and resolved not to let anyone call him Bolbol anymore. A heavy silence settled in the car. No one asked Bolbol any questions, and they kept Fatima's muteness from him. His uncle exchanged a glance with his cousin; they were wondering about his sanity. His vacant eyes, trembling hands, and twitching body all indicated that something traumatic had happened to him overnight. Bolbol understood and assured them that the only reason for his appearance was the biting cold, saying that he would soon recover. When he reached the 'aza, the women started crying again. Weeping, Fatima rushed toward him and embraced him. She tried for the last time to recover her voice, and her sobs grew louder when she realized she still couldn't speak. Muteness had taken total possession of her. Bolbol wished it had been him rather than Fatima; he envied her eternal silence. Still, he was moved at having finally arrived; he felt great gratitude for being among people who were able to protect him. It had been a long time since they had left Damascus.

Hussein was ignoring him, which hurt. He'd considered it sufficient to ask Bolbol briefly if the extremists had tortured or harassed him. All Bolbol could hear in these questions was his brother saying *I hate you*, so he made do with a brief gesture of dismissal and returned to gazing into a far corner of the spacious but cozy guest room.

Bolbol bathed in warm water, and his cousin gave him clean pajamas. He ate dinner with everyone but kept silent, surrounded by sympathy on every side. When he lay down in bed, he was assailed by nightmares; he felt he was hanging from the ceiling of a wide room, flying in a narrow space, crossing a nearby border, and beginning a new life. Despite the nightmares he was able to sleep for a few hours and woke up at dawn. He didn't yield to the temptation of remaining in the warm bed but got up at once and walked to the graveyard with his cousin. He stifled his anger when he saw his father's grave had been dug at a distance from all the others. He hadn't been buried beside his sister's grave, and so his last wish had not been carried out after all. Nor, indeed, had he been buried near his mother or his grandmother. The grave was isolated in a distant corner of the graveyard. He had lived at a distance and had to be buried at a distance—but in the end he had a grave, and that was no trivial thing. They didn't linger; Bolbol stayed just long enough to uproot some dead weeds from his mother's grave. He felt an overwhelming grief; perhaps she'd never known that she hadn't meant anything to his father, that she had been just a wife. Everything that had been said about their great love story had been a lie no one dared to refute even now; the living had to keep telling hypocritical stories about the dead. Bolbol didn't protest or wonder why they had buried him so far from his loved ones. He thought, later, that a distant grave was the truest, most appropriate one for his father. His aunt hadn't wanted anyone from her family to share her grave; she had wanted a solitary resting place, where no one would dare to sleep but her. Her legend grew day by day, exciting the imagination and widening the distance between herself and the living. Many had considered moving or even destroying her grave, but none of the living dared to raise a finger. Even her brother Nayif, the last witness, hadn't been brave enough; he asked everyone to be content to forget. The story would endure, and any attempt to erase it would only reignite it. Layla shouldn't be turned into the patron saint of lovers. She should be left to lie quietly in oblivion, without notice, in a neglected grave without a marker.

On the morning of their third day in Anabiya, Bolbol decided to cross the border to Turkey. One of his cousins drove with him in case he needed any help. The crowd at the Bab al-Salamah crossing was frighteningly large; thousands of people were waiting to cross. Bolbol thought then that his desire to start a new life was basically just another lie; he knew he was too weak to manage it.

A new life meant a new unknown, and that required strength. He missed his house, and the repetitive moments of his work and his office, his pickles, his fear of the fascists who raised their rifles and wanted to plow through Deraa and plant it over with potatoes. His cousin sensed his confusion; his expression changed, and he suggested they go back to Anabiya and think again. He took Bolbol by the arm and drew him away. He was starting to be convinced that Bolbol had lost his mind; he couldn't let him cross the border when his silent face showed plainly that he couldn't tolerate the consequences of such a decision. On their way back to Anabiya, Bolbol's cousin assured him that they could help him to cross into Turkey any time he liked.

At dawn on the fifth day, their cousins accompanied the three siblings to the outskirts of Aleppo. The checkpoints were all opened to them, and the journey was easy. They bid each other goodbye at the last checkpoint before his cousins turned around to go back. The siblings felt relieved and cheerful; they had carried out their father's last wish, and they weren't carrying a body with them. A long silence settled over the three of them. Fatima was content to sleep all the way back. No longer able to speak or nag, she, too, wanted to go back to her house. Hussein and Bolbol ignored each other.

When they reached Damascus in the evening, Bolbol got out of the minibus and raised his hand in a wordless farewell to Hussein. He had appreciated his silence. His neighborhood wasn't far, and he walked back through the shadows along the Corniche Highway. It was nine o'clock when he opened his front door. The smell of his father wafted through every nook of the house. Bolbol sat there in darkness. He felt more alone than he had ever felt. He resolved not to let anyone call him anything other than his original name, Nabil, from now on. He felt as though his head had been gnawed by the dogs that had attacked them and that he, too, was now just a cadaver. He got up and put his head under the hot-water tap. He wanted his features to melt and disappear. His silence would last all night. He walked to his bedroom, slipped into bed, and felt like a large rat returning to its cold burrow: a superfluous being, easily discarded.